Lucas Lightfoot
AND THE
SUN STONE

LUCAS LIGHTFOOT and the SUN STONE

Copyright © 2022 by Hugo Haselhuhn and Luke Cowdell
Cover Art © 2022 Haselhuhn Design, Inc

Epigrams at the beginning of each chapter are quotes selected from the **Book of Prescottian Wisdom**.

Graphic Illustrations: Isabeau Bradshaw
Cover Illustration: Ana Grigoriu-Voicu
https://www.books-design.com/
Title Font: Romance Fatal Serif © Juan Casco, Used with permission

Lucas Lightfoot and the Sunstone
Published by Haselhuhn Design Inc.
ISBN: 978-0-9912439-3-8 Paperback
ISBN: 978-0-9912439-4-5 eBook

All rights reserved. No part of this book may be reproduced by any mechanical, photographic or electronic process, or in the form of phonographic recording, nor may it be stored in a retrieval system, transmitted, or otherwise copied for public or private use – other than for "fair use" as brief quotations embodied in articles and reviews without prior written permission from the publisher, Haselhuhn Design Inc.

This is a work of fiction. Although some of the elements in this story may appear to be biographical, the names, characters, businesses, places, events and incidents are either the products of the authors' imagination or used in a fictitious manner. Any resemblance to real persons, living, dead or anywhere in between is purely coincidental.

The text type is 12-pt. Maiandra GD

This book is dedicated:

To all the children who find it easy to imagine themselves in the magical world of adventure with Lucas and Hailey.

To all the adults who read with their children, so they can relive the childhood fantasies through these adventures.

To all young readers and those who are young at heart who believe they can make a difference in the lives of children.

CONTENTS

Preface vi
Acknowledgments ix
One			Light Thief 1
Two			Hero's Path 5
Three		Fresh Recruits 11
Four			Surprising Revelation 19
Five			Light Academy Teachers 38
Six			Intelligence Power 58
Seven		Truth or Consequences 71
Eight		Shape Shifting........................... 80
Nine			African Race of Life 91
Ten			English Statues 110
Eleven		Fallen Stones 124
Twelve		The Vanishing Wolf 132
Thirteen		Results of Initiative 146
Fourteen		Leaving Normal Behind............ 158
Fifteen		Reality is Simply an Illusion....... 168
Sixteen		Quest for the Sun Stone........... 182
Seventeen	Time is Running Out................. 192
Eighteen		A Very Sad Movie 201
Nineteen		Leap of Faith in Time............... 208
Twenty		Stormy Weather 219
Twenty-One	Sun Stone and Light Power 225
Twenty-Two	In the Arms of an Angel........... 240
About the Authors 261

Preface

Our first book, _Lucas Lightfoot and the First Crystal_, started when my grandson had a dream to write a "chapter book." I am grateful to Luke and his mother, Heather Cowdell, who encouraged her son to accomplish his dreams.

In _Lucas Lightfoot and the Water Tomb_, the adventure continues for Lucas Lightfoot with elements from the childhood of a grandfather and his grandson. Luke and I collaborated on general ideas for the story. Luke told me where he wanted to go and I provided the road, created the characters and painted the scenery along the road they traveled.

Now, in our third book, _Lucas Lightfoot and the Sun Stone_, Lucas learns he has been given the birthright to possess the power of the Sun Stone, yet he doubts whether he is ready to accept the responsibility that comes with that power. He has mentors and teachers who offer training and knowledge, but there are evils forces that want to steal the power and light from Lucas. With his friend, Hailey, Lucas travels to Africa, England and Spain to secure the keys to unlock the Sun Stone concealed in a temple in Thailand. Come with Lucas, Hailey and the magical chameleon, Prescott, as they discover the hidden lessons found in every country they visit and confront the enemy at every turn. With their permission, I have created characters and named them after children and teachers I have met in classrooms and at book signings. Students in Mrs. Moore and Ms. Miller's classes asked that I include their teachers in the Sun Stone. Sandy and Cindy have been Lucas Lightfoot cheerleaders from the very start and are now special teachers on the pages of _Lucas Lightfoot and the Sun Stone_.

Author's notes and comments about Lucas Lightfoot

Why do I write? It began as a way to help a grandson achieve a dream. As I continue to write, it is because I want to improve the lives of children. Throughout the story, my goal is to teach the importance of choice and accountability, the value of learning and improving the mind, importance of attitude and belief in one's ability to help others. Integrity and honesty are still valuable traits to develop and hold dear. There is value in love, understanding and gratitude in our lives. These values are critical for a rising generation that is bombarded with anti-heroes that exemplify the opposite traits of selfishness, falsehoods, power-seeking and bullying. The lessons are conveyed just beneath the natural conversations of the characters while the reader is drawn into the excitement that comes with the challenges and adventures in the story. I marvel as I watch children read the story and get excited as they are caught up in the adventure and excitement. Thanks to Tony Robbins, I have included elements of NLP, Neuro-Linguistic Programming, to help children develop skills to navigate their world and improve their ability to increase emotional resiliency. If I can enlighten a child and take them on an adventure they enjoy again and again, I am successful in my writing. Why do I write? I write to improve the world, one child at a time.

The authors, Hugo Haselhuhn and Luke Cowdell, have spoken in classrooms, at school assemblies and were the keynote speakers at the Utah Literacy Council. The authors are available speak in schools on topics and values from the books: _Put More M.A.G.I.C. In Your Life_ is a presentation on the Mind, Attitude, Goals, Integrity and Choice. Hugo Haselhuhn has also created and presented a Writers Workshop for children, and he is available to present classroom, school assembly or writers' workshops for schools. More information is available on the website: www.lucaslightfoot.com.

Acknowledgments

"From the moment I received the first Lucas Lightfoot book in the series, I have read the books every year to my students. This book series is a gift of pure M.A.G.I.C. that has to be shared. In a world filled with darkness, the Lucas Lightfoot series provides heart-warming, adventurous stories that encourage readers to live virtuously and shine brightly. According to the authors, it is M.A.G.I.C. - Mind*Attitude*Goals*Integrity*Choice. Hugo and Luke wrote the text and I get to share the light and guide my own students to notice and discover their own inner power that inspires them to be the best they can be."
Jenny Stephens ~ 3rd Grade Teacher, Tustin, CA

"We had the pleasure of having Mr. Haselhuhn at a wonderful assembly. I had just finished reading Lucas Lightfoot and the Fire Crystal to my class as a read aloud. What a great book! There were many talking points and opportunities to discuss students' ability to be powerful and successful in their own lives by making excellent choices and setting goals. My students were highly interested and engaged in the discussions. This book will be a part of my routine for the beginning of the school year every year!
Cheryl Elisarraraz, ~ 4th Grade Teacher, Paso Robles, CA

"I was hooked from the start with the vivid descriptions, intrigue of a talking chameleon guiding the young hero, and page turning suspense. As a parent and teacher, I was captured by the action and integrity. The book speaks to children. It is relatable. Kids love powers and superheroes. Better yet, parents and teachers are attracted to this young book hero who has powers that are activated and strengthened by virtues. The power of communication and understanding of dialogue between light bearer and animal is a real draw for kids. Kids love animals. The author has a knack for kid connection. *Lucas Lightfoot and the Water Tomb* is sure to engage the audience of today's youth while teaching lessons throughout the plot and building character simultaneously. It is like the perfect ice cream sundae with goodness and unselfish acts as the nuts and cherry on top. This book is an adventurous treat for children and adults alike. Find a young friend and read it together."
Sandi Moore ~ 3rd Grade Teacher, Templeton, CA

"My students used adjectives like "hypnotizing," mysterious," and superb" to describe the story they previewed. Young readers will be captivated by the plot of the story, but they won't fail to recognize that the goodness in Lucas's heart is the true source of his power. This book is perfectly suited for the minds and hearts of children."
Cindy Miller ~ 3rd Grade Teacher, Templeton, CA

"I am especially grateful to my editor, Patricia Alexander, for her careful editing to create a polished manuscript. Patricia has been a tremendous help in bringing clarity and honesty to my writing and my characters. She has a keen ear and listens carefully for emotions, sentence structure and appropriate language for the intended reader. Working with Patricia has helped me take a good story and make it great."

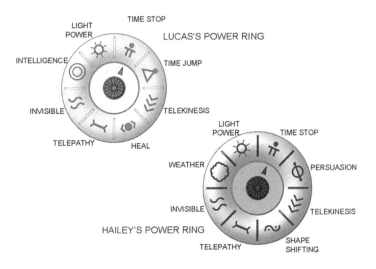

Visit the Lucas Lightfoot website to see the interactive Power Rings and to rotate them in 3D at www.lucaslightfoot.com

ONE

Light Thief

The worst prison is a closed heart.

Rebulus the Light Thief hunched over a walnut-size stone he held in the palm of his deformed hand. He had an extra finger on each hand and the fingers were permanently curled inward. Barefoot and shirtless, Rebulus wore only a pair of tattered brown pants. His hairy body served as his shirt. His head was overly large for his four-foot height and the marble-size bumps covering his body added to his ugly appearance. He could rarely sneak up on someone because of his odor. The sulfur smell of rotten eggs announced his approach. He could easily win an ugly creature contest. He rarely went outside, but when he did, he enjoyed the look of fear in the eyes of those who saw him.

The moon stone he was holding gave off a yellow glow, bright enough to reflect off the water trickling down the wall of a remote cavern of Dragon Caves. He liked the darkness this cavern provided. Here he did not need to be hidden by the cloud that often became his cloak when he

went outside. Rebulus was different. He was born with a deformed body and no amount of magic could change that, *unless... unless* he could get his hands on a Power Ring. He was angry that his mother had failed him. The one person who should have loved him the most left him behind when she disappeared. His father, Vilonious, was left to raise him. Rebulus learned his mother was a Light Bearer, and because he thought she had abandoned him, he grew to despise all Light Bearers. Vilonious taught Rebulus to seek for power and control by any means possible. Vilonious told him that with a Power Ring, he could change into anything he desired. His father had devised a plan to obtain the greatest Power Ring so Rebulus could be freed from his disfigured body. Rebulus had hatred for all Light Bearers, but that loathing became absolute, when Liam Kincaid and the leaders of the Light Bearers, had killed his father Vilonious when he tried to steal the Sun Stone.

Thunder shook the ground and the sound echoed through the tunnels of the cave as a reminder of the violent storm raging outside. Rebulus scowled and clenched his jaw as if he had eaten something bitter. His right eye began twitching again.

Rebulus thought about his beautiful Senka and how much he missed her. Senka had the ability to change her appearance at will. At times, she appeared as a lovely young woman with long black hair. But Rebulus loved her best when she would change into a beautiful and fierce wolf. He had promised her power, power they could use to satisfy their greed, but now she was gone and Rebulus was angry. He was angry because Lucas was responsible for her disappearance. Was she dead? Had she been taken somewhere? Was she in hiding? Rebulus did not know. There it was again. Every time he thought about Lucas, his right eye started twitching.

Rebulus especially hated Lucas because he had outsmarted his beautiful Senka. She was supposed to take the Power Ring from Lucas, and she almost succeeded. Senka was smart and clever, but maybe over confident. Rebulus was sure that Lucas, an ordinary boy, was responsible for her disappearance somewhere in the desert. There was nothing Rebulus could do so he decided to not worry about her. He had others he could use to get what he wanted. Rebulus had summoned the twins.

TWO

Hero's Path

*The bridge between knowledge and skill is practice.
The bridge between skill and mastery is time.*

"Okay Lucas. Lights out, it's time to sleep. Did you remember that Grandpa will be here tomorrow morning?" asked his mom.

"Oh yes, how could I forget? But can I please finish this chapter in my book? It's only three more pages."

"Okay, just three more pages and then off to sleep you go," agreed Lucas's mom. "Good night."

"Good night, Mom. See you in the morning."

Lucas finished reading but was not thinking about the words on the page. He was thinking about Grandpa. Lucas always looked forward to visits with Grandpa Jack, especially since he learned that his grandfather was a Light Bearer like himself. Lucas thought about how much his life had changed since that amazing day when he found Prescott on the sidewalk.

Prescott, the magical chameleon, had actually chosen Lucas because there was a light inside Lucas that made him different from most children his age. Lucas just thought of himself as an ordinary boy with dreams of doing something extraordinary. He and Prescott quickly became close friends and Prescott found ways to show Lucas just how special he could be. Lucas closed the book, put it on his desk and turned out the light. The glow-in-the-dark stars glued to the ceiling gave off faint green light, especially the stars above the desk lamp.

"Good night, Prescott."

"Good night, Lucas."

It was late but Lucas could not sleep. The single nightlight in his room cast a strange shadow on the wall from the clothes Lucas had left on the chair. The shadow reminded him of Senka howling at the moon.

Lucas lay in his bed considering Prescott's warning about the coming battle. This was not so much a battle of armies with guns between countries for land, but a battle between light and dark. It was a battle between Light Bearers and Dark Runners. That's what Grandpa Jack had called Senka, a Dark Runner. There was little comfort when Lucas reminded himself it was the flash flood that killed Senka, but somehow, he felt responsible.

Outside a steady wind-driven rain was beating on the window. Lucas tried to relax and focused on the sound of the rain, hoping it would calm him so he could sleep. Suddenly there was an incredibly bright flash of lightning through the curtains and the ear-splitting boom of thunder rattled the window. The moment he heard the thunder, a chill ran through his body and a frightening feeling of dread came over him. It was as if something dark and terrifying was coming for him.

"Prescott, are you here?"

"Yes Lucas, I am." assured Prescott in a soothing voice.

"I felt something very scary just now," whispered Lucas. "Did you feel it too?"

"Indeed, I felt what you did," responded Prescott. *"Unfortunately, there are dark forces in the world that do not want you or anyone else to be trained as a Light Bearer."*

"Could there be more Dark Runners like Senka?" asked Lucas.

"Sadly yes, there are more. It seems it is the Dark Runners that do the foul work of Rebulus and others like him, so they can hide in the shadows. The Dark Runners want something you have. They want your light," explained Prescott calmly.

"Are they all wolves like Senka?" asked Lucas.

"Oh no," replied Prescott. *"The Dark Runners can appear as an animal or as a person. Or they can be like Senka who had control over her appearance and could look like a wolf or a woman."*

"How will I ever know if someone is a Dark Runner?" questioned Lucas wrinkling his brow with concern.

Then, as if to answer his own question, "I got it," exclaimed Lucas excitedly. "It would be a whole lot easier if they all had a name tag that said, 'Hi, my name is Dark Runner and I'm here to steal your light.'"

Prescott laughed. *"I wish I could arrange that for you. For some, you will know when they try to harm you. There will be others though, who will befriend you first and then strike when you least expect,"* Prescott then added with encouragement. *"You will need to rely on your heart to warn you, Lucas. Trust your heart."*

Lucas thought about how he was learning to feel and trust with his heart and his thoughts turned to his grandpa. Lucas was excited that Grandpa Jack would be coming tomorrow as he was saving up a lot of questions he hoped his grandfather could answer.

Lucas could feel the cool air flowing down from the closed window above his bed and pulled the covers up around his head. He wanted to sleep but his mind was racing from one thought to another when he heard Prescott call his name.

"Lucas?"

"Yes Prescott, what is it?"

"Do you remember what you wanted to be before we met?"

"Sure," grinned Lucas. "I wanted to be a superhero."

"That is correct," said Prescott, *"You are different now than you were a year ago. And you will be different a year from now because of your experiences. You have been given the power to be a "super" hero when you use the power for good. Did it not feel wonderful when you were able to save Anna from the fire and Hailey from the snakes?"*

"I know. That part feels good. But I didn't know it would be so hard to be a hero."

"I agree. Being a hero is not easy. Your grandfather is a Light Bearer and you have seen just a little of what he can do," reminded Prescott.

"Yeah, but it looks so easy for him."

"It looks easy because he has years of experience," explained Prescott. *"When you practice doing something over and over, it becomes easier. Not because the task is less difficult, but your ability to do that task increases. Lucas, it is hard in the beginning, but you have been chosen because of the light within you, and you are only one of a few who can succeed against the darkness."*

"How do you know?" asked Lucas. "I thought you said you can't see the future."

"That is correct, Lucas. I cannot, but I have faith in you, and I know your heart. I believe you will have the wisdom and courage to meet whatever challenge confronts you. Everyone has a higher purpose in life. If you are patient, you will discover your purpose."

"Do you know what my purpose is?" asked Lucas.

"If I told you, it might take away the ability for you to choose your path. Whether you decide to take the hero's path, or return to the life of a normal boy, it must be your choice. Which path will you choose Lucas?" asked Prescott.

Lucas was silent for a while as he thought about Prescott's words. His thoughts turned to Grandpa Jack and the worry he felt earlier melted away. Lucas drifted off to sleep, completely unaware that at that very moment, Rebulus was planning to steal the Power Ring and the light within Lucas.

Three

Fresh Recruits

Be careful choosing friends who promise what they cannot give.

The twins, Tanis and Damian, were snakes born in the darkness of the caverns and they rarely went out into the light of day. These cave-dwelling Rat Snakes lived on a diet of rats and bats. Rebulus knew he could control these reptiles, but he would have to give them something to accomplish what he wanted. He would have to use some of his dark power to change the twins.

The twin snakes slithered up to the cold damp rock where Rebulus had squatted. The soft glow from the moon stone blended their tan, brown and black scales. Their yellow glass-like eyes reflected the glow of the moon stone Rebulus held in his hand. The snakes cautiously eyed the creature who had taken over their home as his own.

"What do you want?" asked Damian, hissing his words. "Why did you call for us?"

"Welcome, friends of the cave," said Rebulus in his gravelly voice. "I have a very important mission for both of you."

"What do you want from us? What is so important to you?" hissed Damian. Each word was slow and spoken with a hiss from his curved mouth.

"There's a boy named Lucas Lightfoot who needs to be taught a lesson," declared Rebulus. "I need you to get close to Lucas and his friend Hailey. You will become their friends and when they least expect it, you must take his Power Ring. I don't care what you do to Lucas and Hailey, just make sure they never bother me again."

"How can we be friends with them? Do they like snakes?" questioned Tanis.

"Hold on!" interrupted Damian. "Before we become friends with anyone, you need to tell us why we would do this for you? What will you give us in return?" asked Damian.

Rebulus closed his eyes for a moment and greedily thought that his power over these snakes would soon lead to power over the naïve Light Bearers. He grinned at the twin snakes and said, "To help you accomplish this task, I have an amazing gift for you. I have the power to change you from a snake into a human."

The twins looked at each other with surprise trying to imagine what it would be like to be human. Rebulus spoke in a soft and cunning tone to let the impact of what he was offering sink into their minds. He felt bitter that he had power to change the snakes to human, but not the power to change himself. He sighed inwardly and told himself to be patient as that would happen soon enough when they brought him the Power Ring.

"In your human form, the world will belong to you! You will discover a new kingdom on two feet that will take you anywhere! You will be given delicious food and never go hungry. You will be able to laugh out loud, run and jump and ride bicycles. And, most importantly, you will be able to communicate enchanting words to control both people and animals. You will get to know Lucas and his friends, and they will never know what you really are. If you bring me his Power Ring, I will allow you to stay in your human form as long as you like. However, if you cannot get the Power Ring, you will change back into snakes forever. You will be Rat Snakes again stuck in this small dark cave unless you do as I ask. Do we have an agreement?"

Tanis and Damian slithered toward one another and began to coil themselves into a spiral around each other's slender bodies. Rebulus watched as they silently communicated, wondering what they might be thinking and if they were going to join his plan to destroy Lucas Lightfoot. Finally, the twins uncoiled themselves and turned toward Rebulus.

Tanis, with her words hissing, asked, "If we deliver the Power Ring to you, we can remain human forever?"

"Yes. That is my offer," promised Rebulus.

"Then we will be your servants and will do as you ask," hissed Damian.

"We will get the ring and deliver it to you," hissed Tanis in agreement.

"Very well," said Rebulus feeling triumphant. "Then let us begin the change."

Rebulus put the glowing moon stone on the rock altar in front of him. He had the snakes slither on top of the altar and coil themselves with Tanis, the female, on the left side and Damian, her brother, on the right side.

An unseen figure hid in the darkness behind the rocks and watched Rebulus as he cupped his deformed little hands on the heads of the snakes. As Rebulus began chanting, the intruder felt a cold stream of air brush past him from the tunnels in the lower cavern. Within moments, Rebulus, Tanis and Damian were all surrounded in a swirling purple fog. The yellow moon stone began glowing brighter and the light surrounding the stone grew more brilliant. Suddenly, tiny bolts of lightning shot out from the stone into the snakes, stinging Tanis and Damian, and causing them to squirm and thrash about.

"Ow!" shrieked Tanis. "What are you doing? You didn't say this would hurt."

"Be still!" commanded Rebulus. "When I am finished you will thank me."

Tanis closed her eyes tight as she grimaced in pain. Damian held still. He was fascinated with this magic and kept his eyes wide open to watch the unbelievable transformation.

Rebulus held their heads close to the stone until the full effect of the change was completed. When Rebulus finished his chanting, the purple fog descended back to the lower tunnels with a whooshing sound as if the cavern was inhaling a huge breath of purple air. The intruder hiding in the shadows was astonished at what he saw. The Rat snakes were gone and, in their place, stood Tanis and Damian in human form.

Where there once were two snakes, stood two normal well-groomed, ten-year-old kids wearing blue jeans, tee shirts and tennis shoes. Tanis and Damian were both very beautiful in their appearance. Rebulus had even given them a magical power so people would be attracted to them and want to be their friends.

Tanis had beautiful blond hair flowing down to the middle of her back. She had emerald green eyes that sparkled in the darkness. Damian also had blond hair and a mischievous grin. His eyes were sparkling yellow and green. Both children looked like they just stepped off the pages of a fashion catalog with their tanned skin and sun-bleached hair, standing straight and tall. Tanis and Damian looked at each other with wide-eyed amazement. They reached out their arms until their hands touched. They began to touch each other's face.

"Look!" exclaimed Tanis excitedly, "I have hands and fingers and arms and hair!" She reached around her head and grabbed a handful of beautiful blond hair and pulled it around her head so she could see it. "And I can talk and not just hiss! I love my voice! Damian, say something – I want to hear your voice."

"Oh, yes!" responded Damian. "We have legs to walk and run. We don't have to crawl in the dirt anymore."

Tanis grabbed the glowing moon stone and ran to a pool of water so she could see her reflection in the water.

"Oh, Rebulus, I'm so beautiful!" exclaimed Tanis. "Thank you!"

Tanis ran back to Damian and wrapped her arms around her brother and spun around in excitement, almost knocking him over.

"Relax Tanis," said Damian as he stopped the spinning. "This is just the beginning. We must keep our part of the agreement. We need to be serious about getting the Power Ring and delivering it to Rebulus."

"You are my finest creation!" exclaimed Rebulus. "Let me look at you, my wonderful children,"

They continued to hold hands as they turned to face Rebulus.

His right eye began twitching again as Rebulus thought of Lucas, and with a stern warning he said, "Don't let me down. You have exactly thirty days to bring me the ring."

"Thirty days? You didn't say there was a time limit," complained Damian.

"Oh, did I forget to mention that? You have thirty days and no more. Lucas is increasing in his strength, and I fear he may have the ability to use his power even without the ring. And if *that* happens, there will be little you can do to stop him!" exclaimed Rebulus.

"Then we'd better get busy," insisted Damian. He was not happy they had a time limit, but he was excited at the chance of remaining human.

"You can count on us to serve you and bring you the Power Ring," exclaimed Tanis. She was giddy with excitement in her new body and her perfect English.

"And serve me you must. If you fail me, you will become rat snakes again," warned Rebulus. "Remember my instructions. My servant is waiting for you at the entrance to the cave. He will take you where you need to go. Now then, children, make your father proud," he added with a persuading grin.

Tanis and Damian smiled at each other and without saying goodbye they turned their backs on Rebulus and hurried off, eager for their new adventure.

Rebulus had to sit down. He was surprised by how exhausted he felt as the cavern seemed to spin around in circles. Changing the snakes had taken more of his power than he expected. But, with the unique gift of being human, he was trusting Damian and Tanis to accomplish the deed. Rebulus knew that snakes had cunning minds and he looked forward to their victory. He did not even want to consider the twins failing him. But if they did, he had a more treacherous backup plan. Rebulus had a spy in a very high position in the council of Light Bearers and if needed, he would use his knowledge to blackmail the Storm Maker. Rebulus suddenly spun around as he heard a sound from a dark corner of the cave.

"Who dares to come uninvited into my home?"

Rebulus quickly flew in the direction of the noise. The intruder tapped twice on a bracelet and in the blink of an eye, disappeared. Reaching the now empty corner of the cave, Rebulus sniffed the air like a dog and saw the faint remains of sparkling dust settling to the ground.

"A Light Bearer! How did a Light Bearer get into my cave?"

Four

Surprising Revelation

Revelation may not come all at once, but as puzzle pieces we must put together.

"Lucas, wake up. Your grandfather will be here soon," said Prescott. *Lucas? It's time to wake up."*

"Oh, right. Thanks Prescott," murmured Lucas as he sat up and began rubbing his eyes. "Hey, yeah, Grandpa Jack is coming." He jumped out of bed and quickly dressed. He wondered why Grandpa Jack was visiting before Christmas but didn't really care. Any reason to see his grandpa was a good enough reason. Lucas then heard Prescott in his head.

"Lucas, there is a reason your grandfather is here. He is going to tell your parents about the real power within the Power Ring. The time has come to let them know why you were chosen to be a Light Bearer," said Prescott.

Lucas had thought about the different ways he could tell his parents the about the Power Ring. He could explain the symbols. He could tell them about some of the things he was able to do with the power. He could even explain how he used the ring to save Prescott and Anna from the school fire. But how could he tell them he had a talking chameleon with special powers! He shook his head. He was certainly glad Grandpa would be the one to explain everything. Still, Lucas was nervous and wondered how his parents would react.

Shortly after Lucas finished his bowl of cereal, he heard his grandpa's car pull into the driveway and ran out to meet him.

"Hello Lucas! How's my little Light Bearer?" asked Grandpa Jack as he gave Lucas a big hug.

"I'm doing good and being good," replied Lucas.

"Wonderful! Could you please take my suitcase into the house and put it in the guest room?"

"Sure, Grandpa."

Lucas grabbed the suitcase and listened to the clickity-clack sound of the wheels following him as he rolled the suitcase up the stone walkway and into the house. From the hallway, Lucas heard his mom, "Hi Dad. It's good to see you. How are you getting along?"

"I'm feeling very well these days," replied Jack heartily.

When Lucas came back to the living room, his mom and dad were talking with Grandpa Jack. Lucas hung around for a while listening to the conversation, but when he realized it was just small talk, Lucas went back to his room to read the last few chapters of *Twenty-Thousand Leagues Under the Sea*. When he finished reading, Lucas came out of his room looking for his grandfather.

"Hey Mom, where's Grandpa?"

"He said he had some errands to run, and he was going to visit an old friend," replied Lucas's mom.

"I didn't know Grandpa had any friends here," said Lucas.

"Your grandpa has been around a long time. He has friends all over the world so I suspect he might have a few here in Southern California," reminded his mom. "He said he might invite someone over tonight after dinner."

Lucas wondered if the person Grandpa was going to invite over had anything to do with telling his parents about the Power Ring. It was a warm day for December, so Lucas took Prescott out of his cage, and they went out to the back yard. Prescott warmed himself in the sun while creeping around in the grass looking for fresh insects. Lucas and Ranger played fetch with a tennis ball. After the ball had reached the limit of sliminess from Ranger's mouth, Lucas sat down next to Prescott and wiped his hands on the grass.

"Prescott, do you know where Grandpa Jack went?"

"*We talked very briefly when your grandfather arrived,*" replied Prescott. "*He said he was going to invite Katrina Wakanda over tonight to help explain the need for Light Bearers to your parents.*"

"How does Grandpa know Katrina?" questioned Lucas. Then he added, "Wakanda? I guess I never heard her last name before. What kind of name it that?"

"If you have not guessed by now, Katrina is a Master Light Bearer like your grandfather," replied Prescott. *"They have known each other many years. And as for her last name, her mother was French-Canadian, and her father was full-blooded Sioux Indian. Like your grandfather, she too has become very skilled as a Light Bearer and has no need of a Power Ring. In fact, her name means, 'possesses magical power.'"*

"I'm not surprised," nodded Lucas. "The first time I met Katrina she seemed to glow. She was also in the hospital room with Grandma Ellie, but I don't think Katrina was sick."

"Lucas, if you do not mind, the sun has gone behind the trees and I would like to go back to my warm cage with the heat lamp," requested Prescott.

"Of course," replied Lucas as he carefully picked up Prescott and went inside the house.

Later that evening, after dinner, the doorbell rang. Lucas opened the door expecting to see Katrina and was surprised to see Hailey and her parents standing on the porch. Lucas must have looked confused when Hailey's mother asked if they might come in.

"Oh sure," said Lucas. "Sorry. Please come in."

As they walked into the house, Lucas looked at Hailey and using mental telepathy, asked, *"What's going on? Why are you here?"*

Hailey shrugged her shoulders and replied in thought, *"I don't know. My dad just told me we were invited to your house tonight."*

Lucas's mom invited Hailey and her parents to have a seat in the living room. The parents sat in the chairs and on the couch while Lucas and Hailey sat on the floor against the wall.

Just as Lucas got comfortable with his back against the wall, the doorbell rang again, and he hopped up to open the door.

"Hello Lucas," greeted Katrina with a big smile. "It is so good to see you again. How are you?"

Lucas stood there with the door open staring at her beautiful green eyes. She had the clear bright eyes of a younger woman, but her silver hair and the creases around her eyes when she smiled suggested, she was as old as Grandpa Jack. Lucas was amazed by the glow surrounding Katrina and he knew she was someone special. For a brief moment Lucas felt like he was transported to a dark place as a picture flashed in his mind. Katrina was putting her arms around him to shield or protect him and he felt a wonderful feeling of unconditional love coming from Katrina. Then, just as quickly as the picture entered his mind, it was gone.

"Are you going to invite me in?" teased Katrina.

"Oh. Yes! Of course," replied Lucas, "please come in."

Lucas followed Katrina into the living room. Grandpa Jack stood up to greet Katrina, gave her a hug and kissed her on the cheek. That surprised Lucas as he had only seen him kiss Grandma Maria.

She had passed away from cancer when Lucas was five and he remembered her extra-long hugs. At the time they seemed too long but now he missed Grandma Maria and having her arms surrounding him. Suddenly, he wondered, if Grandpa Jack was a Master Light Bearer, why he didn't use his power to heal his grandma. Lucas's thoughts were interrupted when he heard Grandpa Jack in his mind.

"Lucas, I did heal Maria many times. I loved her and did not want to lose her, but the time came when I had to let her go. She told me she had other things to do beyond this life and eventually I accepted that her journey in this life had come to an end. This is something I have shared with very few people because it's so special," said Grandpa Jack as he looked over at Lucas.

Lucas gave Grandpa a look of understanding with a nod and a weak smile.

"Everyone, I would like to introduce my friend, Katrina Wakanda," said Jack. "She has been a family friend for many years. In fact, she set me up on a date with my dear Maria."

Hannah was the first to stand and welcomed Katrina with a hug. Katrina greeted everyone as they were introduced. She nodded to Lucas's father and said," Hello Andrew, I believe we have met before."

Andrew remembered meeting her when she offered to give Prescott to Lucas. Andrew looked at Jack, then Lucas and then back to Katrina trying to understand if there was a connection.

Jack turned to Lucas and asked, "Will you please go get Prescott? He should be a part of this conversation."

As Lucas walked to his bedroom, his mother, Hannah, asked, "What's going on Dad? Why is Prescott a part of the conversation?"

Lucas walked back into the room with Prescott on his shoulder and sat on the floor next to Hailey.

Jack began by saying, "First, I want to thank you all for accepting the invitation to my daughter's home tonight. It should not surprise you when I say that Lucas and Hailey are exceptional children. As their parents, I am sure you feel that way too. But you should also know they are children of light."

Jack looked over at Hannah and saw the expression on her face and said, "Hannah, I know you have questions. Please, just listen and be patient and I will explain everything."

"Okay Dad," said Hannah, "please enlighten us."

Jack continued, "Both Lucas and Hailey are special young people and they have been chosen to be trained as Light Bearers."

Ignoring her father's request for patience, Hannah sat forward and asked, "What do you mean they have been chosen? By whom? And what's a Light Bearer?"

"The world has a great need for leaders from this generation of youth who have integrity and honest hearts. Lucas and Hailey have been chosen by Katrina," Jack paused for moment to make sure all were listening, "and Prescott."

Lucas and Hailey saw their parents in almost one identical movement tilt their heads back and open their eyes wide in disbelief at what they had just heard. They all turned to look at Prescott and in that moment everyone in the room heard Prescott's voice in their minds which created even stranger looks on their parent faces as they heard the chameleon speak.

"Good evening, everyone. My name is Prescott. It is such a pleasure to talk with all of you tonight."

Hailey noticed her dad was shaking his head in disbelief. No one dared to say a word while Prescott was talking for fear that speaking would somehow break the magical spell of a *talking* chameleon. Prescott continued to explain why and how he chose Lucas and Hailey. Prescott explained that the traits of a Light Bearer are honesty and virtue. He told them about the Power

Rings Hailey and Lucas each had, and how the crystals inside the center of the rings vibrate at a frequency to magnify the thoughts of the person holding the Power Ring. The more honest and virtuous the Light Bearer becomes, the greater the power they have.

Lucas had never heard Prescott explain it that way before and it caused him to think more about his life and how he needed to live so that he too, could have greater power. Prescott talked for about twenty minutes and shared some of the history of the Light Bearers, some of the powers they had and why more Light Bearers were needed.

When Prescott had finished speaking, Grandpa Jack looked around the room and announced, "My grandfather was a Master Light Bearer and the Power Rings Lucas and Hailey now possess have been handed down by him. Katrina, Prescott and I are all Master Light Bearers."

Jack looked at Lucas's father and said, "Andrew, I don't know if you knew, but your father, John Lightfoot, was also a Master Light Bearer."

"Really? Why did I not know? Why didn't he ever tell me?" questioned Andrew.

"I cannot answer that, but never before has there been one with the double birthright, until Lucas."

"So, what you're saying is because Lucas has two grandfathers who are Light Bearers, he has..." here Andrew hesitated, searching for words, "...a special birthright?" asked Andrew.

"Yes, that is correct. I can tell by your expression this might be a little hard to understand," said Jack as he looked at Andrew. "Maybe I can explain it another way. We are each born with a light inside of us, a spark of goodness. Both John Lightfoot and I were recognized for our light and chosen and trained as Light Bearers. That light was passed to our children, you, and Hannah. As a result, Lucas, your first born, has much more light within him, more than we have ever seen in such a young boy. In the recorded history of Light Bearers, no one as young as Lucas is filled with so much light and power."

"So, what exactly is the birthright?" asked Andrew.

"As your first-born, Lucas has the double birthright of increased light to become a Master Light Bearer," replied Jack. "And, with that increased light, he also has the responsibility to be a leader by bringing light into the lives of others. To become a Master Light Bearer is his birthright," replied Jack.

"What about Hailey?" asked her mom. "Does Hailey have ancestors who were Light Bearers?"

Katrina spoke up. "There are some exceptional children who are just born with goodness and an abundance of light. It's easy to see that Hailey is an extraordinary young lady and worthy to be called a Light Bearer."

Everyone was silent, taking in all that was said. Hailey's parents were certainly not going to disagree with what Katrina had said. Lucas had been looking down at Prescott, who was now in his lap. He was beginning to understand why he felt such a connection to his Grandpa Lightfoot whom he had never met. When he raised his head, he saw all eyes were on him which made him uncomfortable. Lucas was relieved when Grandpa Jack broke the silence.

"Because Lucas and Hailey are young, they would greatly benefit from thorough training as Light Bearers. We are asking your permission to allow Lucas and Hailey to continue training as Light Bearers with other Masters. I would be happy to explain and answer any questions as best as I can."

Mark Sinclair, Hailey's father was the first to speak, "This is a lot to take in and hard to believe. How is this possible?"

"How is what possible?" questioned Jack.

"How is…, what is….," Mark stammered. "I'm not sure what I am asking. How is any of this possible? Is this some type of magic?"

"Mark, I know you are an engineer and look for logical explanations for things. There needs to be order and the laws of nature must be followed. Maybe you can accept the fact that if something appears to be magic, it is just science we do not yet understand. And as science, it follows laws of nature." replied Jack.

"What kind of power do these Power Rings have?" asked Mark.

Jack smiled and said, "Maybe a demonstration will help you believe without having to completely understand the how."

Grandpa Jack looked over at Lucas and Hailey and asked, "Would you like to give your parents an example of what's possible?"

Hailey looked at Lucas and asked, "What should we do?"

"How about telekinesis?" replied Lucas. Then he added, "Ladies first."

She smiled, dipped her head, and graciously said, "Thank you, Lucas."

Hailey stood up and pulled the Power Ring from her pocket, looked around the room and turned the pointer to the symbol for telekinesis. She saw some bottles of water on the counter in the kitchen. She lifted a bottle with her mind and moved it through the air and left it floating in front of her dad just out of his reach.

"You look thirsty Dad. Would you like some water?" offered Hailey with a grin.

Hailey's mother, Mary Sinclair, let out a little laugh at her daughter's politeness. Despite his puzzled look, Hailey saw her dad begin to smile as he nodded his head in agreement.

"Lucas, would you please unscrew the cap on the bottle?" asked Hailey.

"It would be my pleasure," replied Lucas.

Lucas adjusted the pointer on his Power Ring. The cap on the bottle started spinning upward and floated over to the coffee table where it gently landed next to the magazines.

Hailey moved the bottle closer to her dad and he took hold of the bottle.

"Why, thank you, Hailey," said her dad slowly as he chuckled.

Everyone in the room was now laughing.

Andrew Lightfoot looked at Lucas and asked, "What else can you do with the ring?"

Hailey smiled at Lucas and spoke to his mind and asked, *"Should we disappear?"*

He nodded and they both turned their Power Rings to the "double S" and with a smile as the signal they disappeared at the same time.

"Where did they go Dad?" asked Hannah being very concerned about the children.

"They're still here. Your eyes just cannot see them because they are more like energy and less like matter," assured Jack.

The mothers were sitting on the couch. The young Light Bearers walked around the couch and stood behind their mothers. At the same time, they both whispered in their mother's ears, "I love you mom, I'm right here."

Hannah and Mary turned around to see Hailey and Lucas reappear as they hugged their moms.

"Jackson, what kind of magic is this?" asked Andrew with growing uneasiness.

Jack knew when someone called him by this full name he needed to listen for the real question.

"Andrew, I believe your concern is for Lucas and his involvement in what you are seeing as magic. Is that right?" questioned Jack.

"Yes, I guess so," replied Andrew. "I'm sure Hailey's parents feel the same way."

Mark and Mary Sinclair both nodded their heads in agreement.

"As Prescott explained," said Jack, "the Power Ring is less about magic and more about science. The crystal in the Power Ring becomes an extension of the mind of the person holding the ring. If the mind of the user is pure and honest, then the Power Ring works for good. These two rings are tuned to work with the minds of your son and daughter."

"So, is it like a radio that uses a dial to tune to the right frequency of a radio station?" asked Mark.

"That is an excellent comparison," replied Jack. "The thoughts Lucas and Hailey have, are being transmitted like a radio signal and the Power Ring magnifies their thoughts into action."

Mary Sinclair spoke up and asked, "Are you are asking for our permission to have our children be taught by Light Bearers or asking permission to let them have the Power Rings, or both?"

Before Jack could answer, Hannah asked the question that was probably on everyone's mind. "Is what you are asking going to be dangerous in any way to our children?"

This time Katrina spoke up to address Hannah's concern.

"Jack, if you don't mind, I will answer," said Katrina as she looked at the parents. "Both Lucas and Hailey are special children. This is in large part due to you because of the dedication and wonderful commitment you have made in teaching them to be honest. Granted, there are other children who are honest, but your children are special because the light within Lucas and Hailey is on a much higher level. It's what we might consider to be a 'more pure' light."

Lucas could see Katrina's words relaxed his mother and maybe softened her heart. At least, that's what he hoped.

Katrina continued, "I think you are aware this world is not always a safe place for children. There is too much darkness in the world. Lucas and Hailey have gifts that provide them safety from the evil in the world around them. They are smart, they are virtuous, and they have been given these Power Rings that can be used for good. With the Power Rings they can do good in the world. They also have us to watch over them, and to teach and train them to use their new power."

"So, what are you asking us to do?" asked Hannah.

"We are asking that you allow Lucas and Hailey to attend special classes before or after school to train them to use the powers on their Power Ring. There is a teacher at their school who is a Light Bearer, and she will open her classroom so other Masters can come in and teach Lucas and Hailey," replied Katrina. "They will be well cared for and supervised at all times."

"Who is the teacher?" questioned Mary and Hannah in perfect unison.

"Miss Harrison has been watching over Lucas and Hailey at school for the last two years and has been providing us regular updates on their progress," replied Katrina.

"I didn't know Miss Harrison was a Light Bearer!" exclaimed Hailey.

"She is indeed," replied Katrina, "as are the others she will bring to her classroom to give you further instruction."

"Maybe you will feel more comfortable if we agree to a trial period of training and see where it takes Lucas and Hailey," suggested Jack. "If you will agree to maybe, four weeks of training, we can then get back together and discuss if this is something the children may continue."

The parents looked at each other and slowly nodded their heads in agreement. Deep down inside, the parents had some measure of pride that their children were selected for training as Light Bearers. But they were still unsure how this would affect their children.

"I guess that would be okay," said Mary slowly.

"A trial period will be okay with us as well," said Hannah.

"Splendid!" said Katrina. "I will notify Miss Harrison tomorrow."

"So, Lucas, what else can you do with your ring?" asked his dad.

"Only good things Dad," replied Lucas with a smile. "Only good things."

☼ ☼ ☼

Hailey and her family had gone home, and Lucas was in his room when he overheard his mom and Grandpa Jack talking.

"Why didn't you ever tell me you were a Light Bearer?" asked Hannah.

"There were times when I wanted to tell you, but I didn't want to burden you," replied Jack. "There were even times when I had to use my Power to save you."

"When was that?" asked Hannah.

"Do you remember when we went to the ocean? You were about five at the time," replied Jack. "We had walked down to the water, and I let you sit on the wet sand where you were filling your bucket to make a sandcastle. I turned away for just a second to talk with your sister Sophie and a huge wave dragged you out into the ocean. I used the power of telekinesis to lift you up and pull you out of the water."

"I remember that day," said Hannah. "I also remember at the time you said angels must have helped me. So, you were my angel?"

"Yes, I was your angel that day," said Jack as he put his arms around her and gave her a big hug. Hannah began to realize that having Lucas trained as a Light Bearer might turn out to be a blessing in his life.

Five

Light Academy Teachers

The moment you think of yourself as the master and no longer the student, learning ceases.

Lucas could hardly believe it! Miss Harrison, who had been his teacher for the last two years, was a Light Bearer! There must have been little clues he had missed, but looking back, he realized she had taken a close interest in his problems and the struggles he had. Maybe she had even given him greater privileges. When he had disobeyed her and had gone back into the classroom to get Prescott during the school fire, he was sure she was going to punish him or send him to the principal's office. Thinking back, maybe she knew he had gone back to get Prescott and she allowed it because Prescott would never let anything happen to Lucas. For all Lucas knew, maybe Prescott and Miss Harrison had talked about him, and he was given a chance to learn for himself what strength he could find within.

Lucas was certainly excited to go to school on Monday and see Miss Harrison. Lucas and Hailey had a lot to talk about, so they agreed to walk to school together.

When they were out on the sidewalk in front of Hailey's house, Lucas asked, "What did your parents think about what my grandpa and Prescott told them last night?"

"I'm not sure yet. I think they're okay," replied Hailey. "When we got home, they asked me about some of the other symbols on the Power Ring and how I had used them. I told them about talking with the parrots and how they helped get your stolen Power Ring back. When the rattlesnakes were going to attack Kendall, I told them I was able to stop time so the snakes wouldn't hurt her. I wasn't sure if I should say anything else. But I told them I had been bitten by the snakes in the desert when we were riding our quad runners and you were able to heal me. I think they're beginning to see that having the Power Ring is also a way to protect us from getting hurt."

"I got the same reaction from my parents," said Lucas. "I told them I crashed my quad runner in the desert, and I was able to lift it back onto the trail. I didn't tell them about Senka. I don't want them to worry."

"You are probably right," agreed Hailey who added excitedly, "What do you think about Miss Harrison being a Light Bearer?"

"I think it's awesome," replied Lucas. "I think it's cool that we're invited to attend special classes with other Light Bearers. I wonder who these other Light Bearers are."

"What do you think these classes are about?" asked Hailey.

"I guess it's to learn how to use the other powers on the ring or maybe there are some hidden powers we don't know about," replied Lucas excitedly.

"Sure," said Hailey smiling. "Maybe your secret power is to have intelligence and be as smart as me?"

"Yep, that's got to be it," smiled Lucas. He was not jealous that Hailey was so smart. In fact, it was nice to have someone to share ideas.

When Hailey and Lucas walked into the classroom, Miss Harrison smiled at them and motioned for them to come to her desk.

"I would like the two of you to stay after class this afternoon," said Miss Harrison with a smile. "We have much to discuss."

☼ ☼ ☼

Lucas and Hailey ate lunch at their usual table and Mallory, Lucas's neighbor, came and sat with them. Mallory was their friend, but she had no idea of the magical world all around them. Lucas and Hailey shared a quick glance, acknowledging that they were going to be especially careful about what they said. Lucas hoped they could stay away from any questions about Mallory's Aunt Senka. Her death would have to remain a secret between Lucas and Hailey. Lucas did not get his wish as Mallory was more excited than usual today.

"Guess what?" exclaimed Mallory excitedly. Without waiting she answered her own question.

"There's new information about my missing aunt. My great uncle who lives in England, hired a private investigator to find Senka. My dad contacted the police when Senka didn't come home after four days. We were very worried about her," said Mallory. "I think it was around Thanksgiving when you both went camping in the desert."

Lucas did not want to talk about Senka, but now that he heard the police were involved, he wanted to know more.

"Oh? What have the police found out about her disappearance?" asked Lucas taking out his peanut butter and jelly sandwich.

"So far, they don't have anything specific," said Mallory munching on an apple slice. "Except they know she got on a bus that went to Barstow. They have a color video from a security camera at the bus station in Barstow which shows her getting off the bus with her black and red backpack. Another video shows her standing outside the bus station and looking around like she's waiting for someone. After a few minutes, the video shows her talking with a tall man."

"Do the police know who the man is?" asked Hailey casually.

"No. That's just it! He has white hair, and he might have a beard or mustache, but he always has his back to the camera so the police couldn't see his face to identify him."

"Do you know why she went to Barstow?" asked Hailey, putting carrot sticks in the middle of the table for everyone to share.

"All she told my parents was someone had offered her a job and she was going to be well paid. She said she would be back in a few days," replied Mallory.

"Are there any other clues?" asked Lucas.

"The only other thing we've heard is that a park ranger found a black and red backpack which matches the one Senka was carrying. Get this! All the clothes she was wearing in the surveillance video were *in* the backpack."

"Wait, what! Where did the park ranger find the backpack?" asked Hailey, with raised eyebrows.

"He found it about ten miles northeast of Barstow near a ghost town," replied Mallory. "They found it on the ground behind some rocks."

"Gee Mallory, I hope you find your aunt," said Lucas. It was the only thing he could think of to say to offer some comfort to Mallory. But he knew the truth that no one would ever find the Senka who Mallory knew. Just then the bell rang signaling the end of lunch. Lucas got up immediately as was he eager to go back to class and away from talk of Senka.

☼ ☼ ☼

Lucas kept his head down and tried to focus on his class work the rest of the day. He didn't say much as he was lost in his own thoughts about Senka being buried under the sand and rocks in the middle of the riverbed after the flashflood. He hoped the riverbed was still dry. He wondered if the private investigator would be able to discover where the wolf was buried. And if he did, would he just find a wolf carcass? Lucas told himself not to worry but it did not help. What if Senka the wolf transformed back into a woman somehow? What if another storm came and washed away the sand and rocks and left Senka out in the open and someone found her?

"Lucas! You need to stop worrying!" Lucas heard Hailey in his mind. Her reminder was enough jolt him again to focus on his class work.

He was glad when the bell rang at the end of the day. Everyone was packing their books and homework into their backpacks and rushing to get out the door. Mallory noticed that Lucas and Hailey were not getting up.

"Hey Hailey, aren't you guys going home?" asked Mallory.

"Miss Harrison asked us to stay after school," replied Hailey.

"What's wrong? Are you guys in trouble?" asked Mallory.

"I don't think so," said Hailey. "I will let you know tomorrow."

"Okay, see you later," replied Mallory over her shoulder as she left.

After everyone had gone, Miss Harrison walked over to close the door and lock it. She then closed all the curtains so the only light in the room came from the fluorescent lights in the ceiling.

Miss Harrison turned to Lucas and Hailey. "Katrina called me this morning and said you were ready to begin your new training."

"How come you never told us you were a Light Bearer?" asked Hailey.

"Because I was given the assignment to watch over both of you. I was to record your progress at school to see how you acted and how you treated others. I was happy to report that Prescott and Katrina have chosen well."

"Who did you report to?" asked Hailey. "Is there a President of the Light Bearers?"

"There is a Light Bearer Council that includes seven Master Light Bearers. I was happy to report to them, that in my opinion, you are both ready to continue some advanced training."

Hearing that, Lucas and Hailey grinned at each other. "Can you tell us what we are going to learn?" asked Hailey.

"I don't know everything you will learn, but it's much more than learning to use the Power Ring," said Miss Harrison. "It's about learning to build character, to be unselfish and to serve others. Each of the seven council members have chosen young people, like yourselves, to be trained."

"Who are the members of the Light Bearer Council?" asked Hailey.

"You have already met three. Lucas, your Grandpa Jack is a member. Prescott is a member of the council and so is Katrina. You will be given the opportunity to meet the other four members of the Council and learn from them. You will also be able to learn from your own challenging experiences."

"What do you mean?" asked Hailey.

"What we learn from our experiences has a lot to do with our attitude and how we choose to look at the situation. It's not so much *what* happens to us but *how* we respond to what happens to us, how we act, what we say and what we do. With the right attitude, even a bad situation can turn into a good learning experience."

There was a knock at the classroom door. Miss Harrison walked over, opened it, and the afternoon sun flooded the room. She invited two women to come in and then closed and locked the door with an audible click, yet the room was still as bright as if the door was still open. As the women entered the classroom, Lucas felt a warm breeze that he could almost see. He was surprised as he could feel all his senses come alive and he knew there was something very special about these Light Bearers.

After some brief hugs, Miss Harrison turned and said, "Lucas and Hailey, I'd like you to meet Miss Miller and Mrs. Moore. They are both very special teachers and have come to give you additional training to help you learn to develop and control your powers. They will also be the ones to introduce you to the members of the council."

Lucas looked at Miss Miller and exclaimed, "It's you! You're the substitute librarian who gave me the Lightfoot Family book!

Lucas then realized she probably knew everything that happened in the library, the day he realized he was being a bully to Kevin.

Miss Miller smiled and said, "It's alright, Lucas. I can see you've come a long way since that day in the library."

Miss Miller had reddish brown hair with blonde streaks and when she walked over to shake hands with Lucas, she moved with purpose. Lucas had the impression that Miss Miller was confident and self-assured and nothing or no one would distract her from her goals. He was surprised that all these thoughts about Miss Miller flooded his mind.

She had a firm grip as she shook hands with Lucas and Hailey. "I'm happy to see both of you again and I'm excited to help you in your training," said Miss Miller.

Mrs. Moore had brown shoulder-length hair with bangs that floated just above her eyes. She had a warm smile that could melt the snow and maybe bring an end to winter. He expected to shake hands with her but instead, Mrs. Moore gave Hailey a hug. As she turned toward Lucas, she looked deep into his eyes. She was not reading his mind, but she seemed to be able to read his heart. He saw that her eyes sparkled with the colors of a rainbow. What really amazed him were her pupils. While most people had round black pupils, hers were in the shape of a heart. All he could do was to stare at her eyes. When she hugged him, he felt all his fears evaporate and he was surrounded with pure love. The only other time he had felt that way was when he was hugged by Grandma Maria. When Mrs. Moore stepped back, Lucas felt like she had given him a new power but had no idea what it might be.

Lucas simply said, "It's an honor to be in the presence of royalty."

He was surprised when the words came out of his mouth. He remembered Prescott saying the more he used the Power Ring, the greater the understanding he would have. He instinctively knew there was something special about these teachers. Lucas looked over at Hailey who seemed to be enchanted by the presence of these new teachers as well.

"Lucas and Hailey, it's time to begin your studies," said Miss Harrison. "I will let these two wonderful teachers begin. Maybe Miss Miller can start by sharing some of her thoughts."

"Thank you, Lauren," said Miss Miller. "Let me begin by telling you about the Light Academy. Hailey, I know you like to ask questions because you're curious, but please be patient and all your questions will be answered."

"Are you reading my mind?" asked Hailey.

"No. You must first give me permission, remember? But I can see the excitement of learning in your eyes," replied Miss Miller.

"Your parents have agreed to one hour of "tutoring" sessions after school a few days each week," said Miss Miller. "There are several ways we will teach you. We will teach you how to use your Power Rings. We will also introduce you to other Master Light Bearers and the students they are teaching. And finally, you will receive an assignment that will test your ability to use all the skills and knowledge you have learned and will learn."

"What's the assignment?" asked Lucas.

"That will come from the Council when the time is right," replied Miss Miller. "The Light Academy was started by Master Light Bearers to share their knowledge and to instruct the new generation on how to bring more light into the world by their example. There are Master Light Bearers all around the world and each of them has selected someone just like you. You will have the opportunity to meet and talk with other Masters and their students."

"Does that mean we get to travel?" asked Hailey eagerly.

"Yes, but we will not be traveling in the way you think. It will be what we call virtual travel," replied Mrs. Moore. "Miss Miller and I will be your guides as you visit other Masters and learn from them."

"Virtual travel?" asked Hailey, clearly baffled.

"You will remain in the classroom, but you will have the experience of a virtual reality in your mind as if you are going to another country," replied Mrs.

Moore. "And you will experience sights, sounds, smells and feelings as if you were actually there."

Hailey was visibly thrilled as she raised her hand and asked, "Ooh! Where are we going first?"

"Slow down!" laughed Miss Miller. "You will first need your passports."

"Passports?" asked Lucas.

Mrs. Moore reached into her brown leather bag and pulled out a polished wooden box. She set the box on top of the desk and slid the top of the box off to reveal two metallic bracelets.

She looked at Lucas and Hailey and said, "Please hold out your right arms."

Lucas and Hailey obediently held out their right arms. Mrs. Moore opened the bracelets under the oval symbol that looked like a sun. When she placed them on their wrists, they heard a sound of a quiet click as the open ends of the bracelet closed together. The bracelets appeared to be made from a smooth silver material but with a transparent quality. Lucas turned his wrist over to see how the bracelet was locked together but could not find a seam. It was as if the bracelet was now one continuous circle.

Mrs. Moore sensed his question and said, "The passport is a blend of titanium, niobium and some very special crystals added to give the band a seamless connection. The crystals add special powers to the bracelets. These bracelets are your passports, and they will allow you to take virtual trips to other places around the world."

"What does the sun symbol on the top of the bracelet mean?" asked Lucas as he started fidgeting with his passport.

"The sun symbol is similar to the sun symbol on your Power Rings," replied Mrs. Moore. "But I think you have another question about wearing a bracelet. Am I right Lucas?"

"Well," said Lucas, looking embarrassed and shifting his weight from side to side, "I do think it's kind of girlish for guy to be wearing a bracelet like this," responded Lucas as he looked up into Mrs. Moore's amazing eyes. "I just don't want someone making fun of me."

"They won't make fun of you if they can't see it," assured Mrs. Moore quietly.

"What do mean?"

"The bracelet looks slightly transparent to you and me, but it's invisible to anyone who is not a Light Bearer. You don't need to worry. Only other Light Bearers will recognize the bracelet and you as a Light Bearer and a friend."

That's when Hailey noticed both new teachers also had on identical bracelets. Hailey exclaimed, "Oh, you're wearing the same bracelets, too! Exactly, how is this bracelet a passport?"

"We'll show you how the bracelets work in a few days, but first we need to work on the next power for each of you," said Miss Miller. "Okay?"

The children nodded, a little disappointed.

"As you know, your Power Rings are slightly different. You have some of the same symbols and there are some that are different," reminded Miss Miller. "Lucas, the next power for you to learn is intelligence and Hailey your new power is shape shifting."

Lucas looked crestfallen. *Intelligence? As a Light Bearer, he already had intelligence – and Hailey got to shape shift? That wasn't fair! Unless it meant he got a super I.Q. Hmm! Now that could be interesting....*

Hailey could not hold back her eagerness. "Oh wow! I really want to learn how this power works! I've heard my dad say he would like to be a fly on the wall to listen to someone's conversation. That would be so awesome!"

Miss Miller was quick to reply. "That would be fine until someone came along with a flyswatter. But fortunately, this power does not work that way."

"How does it work?" asked Hailey.

"With this power," began Miss Miller, "You will have the ability to change your appearance so you will look and sound like someone else, but you will still be Hailey inside. You can only shape shift to look like another human, but not any animal. Always remember, this power, like all the powers, is to be used with integrity and only for the protection of yourself or those you care about. It's not to be used dishonestly or for personal gain."

"How do I turn it on?" asked Hailey.

"First, you must touch the person you want to shift into. When you are ready to shift, turn the pointer on the ring to the "S" symbol with the two dots and focus on that individual while you squeeze the crystal in the ring. When you have mastered your ability to focus and concentrate, you will appear as the person you have selected. And, this is very important, unless the other person is aware you are shifting to look like them, I suggest you get out of their sight, so they are not surprised by seeing a copy themselves."

"Can I try it now?" asked Hailey.

"Yes," replied Miss Miller. "But Hailey, this power will take practice and concentration. It will be best to practice with Lucas or someone in your family who understands this power."

Hailey turned the pointer on her Power Ring to the "S" symbol for shape shifting and focused on looking just like Lucas. She closed her eyes and focused on her friend, but nothing happened.

"What did you forget?" asked Miss Miller.

Hailey opened her eyes and saw Lucas had his hand up ready to give her a "high-five."

"Oh yeah," said Hailey as she reached up and slapped Lucas's hand.

She then squeezed the crystal and focused with determination. Lucas watched the expression on Hailey's face as she concentrated. Slowly at first, Hailey started to appear blurry and out of focus like he had put on someone's glasses with thick lenses. Within a few seconds, Hailey was gone and replaced with someone who looked just like Lucas. He stood in amazement with his mouth open.

Jokingly, Hailey said, "Lucas, your mouth is open."

"You sound just like me too!" exclaimed Lucas.

"You sound just like me too!" replied Hailey.

"Stop it!" said Lucas.

"Stop it!" repeated Hailey.

As they stood there looking at each other, Hailey began copying every move Lucas made. The copycat Lucas made a rather surprising sound and smiled.

"Hey, did you just fart?" asked Lucas.

"I'm doing my best to be just like you," replied Hailey as she started laughing. The laughter caused her to lose concentration and she started to switch back and forth in her appearance until she snapped back to herself. They continued to laugh out loud and even the teachers were laughing.

"What just happened, Hailey?" asked Miss Miller. "Why were you not able to keep the appearance of Lucas?"

"I guess I lost my concentration," replied Hailey.

"That's exactly right," said Miss Miller. "You might find yourself in a situation where it's extremely important you continue to focus on the person into whom you have changed. If you slip up like you just did, you might put yourself and others in danger. You must practice each of your powers until they become second nature. If you practice where it is safe to make mistakes, you will not worry about errors, and it will be easier to develop the skills you need. As you continue to practice these powers, they will become easier to use and will become second nature."

"I think I get it," said Hailey. "I should practice with Lucas or my family where it's okay to make mistakes until I get it right. I should practice until I can be perfect at shape shifting."

"Yes, that's correct," replied Mrs. Moore.

"When do I get to learn and practice my new power?" asked Lucas.

"I'm sorry, Lucas! Our time is gone for today. We'll focus on your new power tomorrow," promised Miss Harrison.

"Wait, what?" exclaimed Lucas disappointedly. "What about my new power?"

Mrs. Moore saw his frustration and calmly answered, "Lucas, the power of intelligence is one of the most important and we do not want to rush this training. You will be able to accomplish great things with it, so we need to work through it slowly."

"Okay, tomorrow then," replied Lucas.

☼ ☼ ☼

"I'm home," called out Hailey as she closed the front door. Hailey found her mom in the kitchen.

"Hi sweetie how was your first day of Light Bearer training?" asked her mom.

"It was so cool, Mom!" exclaimed Hailey excitedly. "We met two really great teachers. One of the teachers showed me how to use the shape shifting power."

"Shape shifting? That sounds dangerous. Are you going to be safe?" questioned her mom.

"Don't worry mom, it's not really dangerous," assured Hailey. "I don't actually shift into someone else. I just appear to be someone else to the eyes of those who see me."

"And I can't shape shift into an animal!" assured Hailey. "I can only appear as another human being."

"How does it work?" asked her mom curiously.

"Miss Miller said that I need to practice with someone I trust until I'm really good at it," replied Hailey. "Can I practice my shape shifting with you?"

"Sure, okay. How does it work?" asked her mom.

Hailey pulled out her Power Ring and turned the pointer to the shape shifting symbol. She then touched her mom's hand and squeezed the crystal. Right before Mary Sinclair's eyes appeared another Mary Sinclair!

"That's amazing! But how is this even possible?" said Mrs. Sinclair as her eyes opened wide in surprise. Her daughter's appearance in height, body size and even down to the brown pants and blouse she was wearing made it look like Mrs. Sinclair was standing in front of a mirror.

"That's amazing! But how is this even possible?" replied Hailey as she began mimicking each of her mother's facial expressions and movements. Her voice even sounded the same.

"Hey, maybe we could make our own Freaky Friday movie," said Hailey, "and surprise dad when he gets home?"

They both began laughing as Hailey lost her concentration and the ability to shape shift. Within moments, the real Hailey Sinclair was standing in front of her mom.

Mary became very serious and said, "Hailey, please be careful and do not let this power get you in trouble. It would be wrong to shape shift and cause someone else harm.

"Don't worry Mom. I will be careful," assured Hailey. Even as she said these words, Hailey began thinking of who she could shift into and what she could learn by being someone else.

Six

Intelligence Power

The real purpose of teaching is not to fill minds with facts and ideas, but to change lives.

The next morning, Lucas and Hailey walked to school together.

"Did you say anything to your parents about our after-school tutoring?" asked Lucas.

"I told them about the new teachers and the shape shifting power. They seemed a little worried about this power so I showed them how I can change. I assured them I'm still me, but I just appear differently to others.

Hailey giggled. "I showed my mom by shape shifting into her."

"No way!"

"It was fun! But I think they understand that the Power Ring is not a toy and only to be used for special purposes. How are your parents?" asked Hailey.

"A little worried – just like yours," replied Lucas. "But they just learned that I have a magical chameleon who can talk. So, after Gavin and

Madison went to bed last night, my dad came into my room and – catch this - he started a conversation with Prescott. I think my dad is interested in the history of the Light Bearers especially when he found out his father was a Master Light Bearer. Prescott shared some stories about my Grandpa Lightfoot my dad had never heard. I think my dad and Prescott are going to get along very well."

Even though they got to class a little early, Mallory was already there. She was clearly excited about something as she motioned for them to come over to her desk.

"You'll never guess what happened," said Mallory excitedly.

"What?" said Hailey and Lucas together.

"The private investigator found paw prints in the dirt where they found the backpack Senka was wearing in the video," said Mallory with wide eyes.

"Paw prints? What kind?" asked Hailey.

Whenever Mallory was excited, she would wave her arms as she talked, and this was one of those times. Lucas wondered if she was pointing to imaginary things only she could see in her mind.

"The park ranger told the investigator he thought the paw prints were too big to belong to a dog, so he brought in a real Native American, a genuine animal tracker! He said they were most definitely wolf prints even though wolves are very rare in that area."

Hailey and Lucas turned to look at each other with concern.

"Uh, do they think Senka was killed by a wolf?" asked Hailey.

"There was no sign of a struggle and there's no blood, so they've ruled out that possibility," replied Mallory. "The private investigator told my dad and great-uncle something incredibly strange. There is only one set of shoe prints in the soft dirt going into the place where they found the backpack, and then, only the wolf prints were seen on the ground going away from the area."

"Maybe Senka had a pet wolf, and she rode on the back of the wolf," speculated Hailey. She was trying to suggest some possibility that would lead Mallory away from the real truth about Senka.

"Now you're just being silly," said Mallory. "I'm really worried about my aunt."

"I'm sorry," said Hailey. "I was just trying to make you smile a little. It must be hard not knowing."

Mallory did not know the truth about her aunt and would probably not believe it if she were told.

"I heard that the investigator is going to start asking around in the neighborhood if anyone had heard or seen my aunt," said Mallory. "After that, he's going to look at the camping permits around the time she disappeared and start interviewing those people."

Lucas started to feel lightheaded. He grabbed for his desk and put the palm of his hand to his forehead.

"What's wrong?" asked Hailey.

"I dunno. I'm just feeling a little sick," replied Lucas.

"Do you want me to walk you to the nurse's office?" asked Hailey. Then using telepathy, she said, *"I'm sure this talk of Senka is upsetting, but we'll get through this. I promise."*

"Thanks, I'll be okay. I just need to sit down."

Just then the bell rang, and Lucas gladly turned his thoughts toward his book report. The rest of the day went slowly for Lucas. He remembered an expression Grandpa Jack used to describe something slow. He would say something was, 'as slow as molasses in the wintertime.' That was a good description for this day. Lucas was anxious to be with Mrs. Moore and Miss Miller after school.

☼ ☼ ☼

At the end of the school day, Lucas and Hailey walked out of the classroom with the other students and then went back a few minutes later so they wouldn't have to explain to Mallory why they were staying after class again.

"Thank you for staying today," said Miss Harrison.

Miss Miller and Mrs. Moore arrived right on time and the door was locked behind them. Mrs. Moore looked at Lucas and immediately asked, "What's wrong Lucas?"

Lucas wanted to spend his time on training with the teachers and not talking about Senka, but he was sure that avoiding the topic with Mrs. Moore would be impossible. And sure enough, before he could say anything, Mrs. Moore gently asked, "Is it about Senka?"

Lucas was a little annoyed. "Why do I need to answer the question if you can read my mind and already know the answer?"

Mrs. Moore assured, "I'm not reading your mind. I'm using my gift. Some people call me an empath."

"What's an empath?" asked Hailey.

"An empath can perceive and identify with the emotions of others. My gift is a natural ability to feel and recognize what others are feeling. By being aware of the energy surrounding them, I can sense their emotions, as well as anticipate what they plan to do."

"That sounds like a wonderful gift," exclaimed Hailey.

"It can be," replied Mrs. Moore. "But it can also be difficult. When I am around sad people who are hurting, I feel their pain as if it were my own."

"Lucas," said Mrs. Moore, "I would like you to consider the difficult situation you faced with Senka. She was trying to take away the Power Ring you were given. She was planning to leave you unprotected so Rebulus could draw the light out of you. She knew that if you had the Power Ring, she could not kill you. If Rebulus had possession of the Power Ring, he would have found a way to use it for evil."

"But I killed Mallory's aunt," said Lucas sadly.

"Did you? Are you sure? She may have been Mallory's aunt, but Senka was given power to change into a wolf and she chose to harm you. Had you considered the possibility that it was self-defense? The flash flood killed the wolf, not you. Senka was trying to kill you and you were only protecting yourself and Hailey."

"Huh! I guess you're right," admitted Lucas slowly.

Mrs. Moore walked closer to Lucas and put her hands on Lucas's shoulders and said, "Please close your eyes."

Lucas closed his eyes. He could feel a tingling in his shoulders, and it felt as if she was pulling something dark from him. After a few moments he felt warmth on his shoulders where Mrs. Moore rested her hands and a feeling of calmness washed over him.

"Wow! What did you do? I feel like a weight has been lifted off me. I feel lighter."

"Wonderful!" said Mrs. Moore. "I'm glad you're feeling better. Lucas, it truly was not your fault. Now, I think you're ready to begin your next lesson. Miss Miller is going to take over for this training."

"Lucas, the next power you're going to learn is the power of intelligence, "said Miss Miller.

"Great! Now I can be as smart as Hailey," said Lucas as he shot her a grin.

Miss Miller smiled. "But, seriously, children. Pay attention now. I will tell you what the Power of Intelligence is and what it isn't. This power will *not* make you smarter by putting facts into your head. This power will *not* raise your IQ, although I'm sure you're both very smart, and it will *not* give you answers on a test for which you have not studied."

Lucas and Hailey glanced over at Miss Harrison and saw her smiling and nodding in agreement.

"Intelligence is more than knowledge. Intelligence is the combination of knowledge, understanding, reasoning, thinking, inspiration and imagination. There is intelligence all around. All you need to do is to tap into it," said Miss Miller.

"What do you mean, 'tap into it.' How do I use the Power Ring to do that?" asked Lucas.

"Imagination is an important part of intelligence," said Miss Miller. "Both of you are already using this power to some degree. Hailey, when the parrots helped recover Lucas's ring, you used creative thinking to imagine how you could solve the problem. Lucas, you knew about flash floods. You used your imagination and judgment to know how to catch Senka off guard and when to run, saving both you and Hailey."

"This power is best used when trying to solve problems or think up new ideas," said Miss Miller. "Look at the situation and think deeply about the problem. Consider the possible causes for the situation and then try to imagine all the possible solutions. When you have thought it through in your mind, turn the pointer to the symbol with the two concentric circles. Squeeze the crystal and ask in your mind, 'what is the best solution to this problem or what is mine to know?' You might be surprised by the answer."

"What do you mean surprised?" asked Lucas.

"Remember, I said there is intelligence all around," replied Miss Miller. "Just because your answer comes from an unexpected source, don't dismiss it. The answer might come from a conversation you have with someone. It might come as you are reading a book. It might even come as a flash of inspiration when you're doing something totally unrelated. Your brain is an incredible computer, but it is often the sub-conscious mind that will find the answers. All you need to do is ask."

Mrs. Moore began to feel some emotions coming from Hailey. It felt like envy, as though Hailey would like to have the intelligence power on her ring too.

"Hailey," said Mrs. Moore softly, "I want you to know that what you have heard from Miss Miller can be done by anyone. You do not need a Power Ring to get access to this intelligence. The

Power Ring only helps to increase the access to the intelligence that's all around."

Hailey nodded, satisfied with the answer from Mrs. Moore to her unasked question.

"Can I practice using this power now?" asked Lucas, trying not to sound too eager.

"Certainly, what problem would you like to solve?"

Lucas thought about some of the problems that were bothering him. Mallory's uncle had hired a private investigator and he might ask questions that could link him to Senka. Prescott had warned Lucas there was going to be a war between the Light Bearers and the Dark Runners. Being called on to be a hero was harder than he expected. These were all tough problems. Maybe he should start with an easy one.

Mrs. Moore was watching Lucas as he thought about his concerns. She began to feel some of the gloom he was feeling. She saw he was looking down and his shoulders started to slump when she asked, "What are you feeling right now Lucas?"

"I don't know, maybe kind of sad."

"Lucas, you are not going to find answers by looking down there."

"What do you mean?"

"When people are sad, they tend to look down with a slouched posture and drop their shoulders," said Mrs. Moore. "The reverse works the same way. If you look down and drop your shoulders, you do start to *feel* sad."

Lucas saw Hailey stand a little taller and he did the same.

"One way to think about intelligence is that it's like a layer of mist floating just above your head. Inside this swirling mist is information. Information you can use to solve problems, create solutions or come up with new ideas."

"So, what do I do?" asked Lucas.

"Stand up straight, look up and smile. When you do this simple physical action, it changes your emotional attitude," replied Miss Miller. "Just imagine the intelligence is swirling all around above you. You will find answers from this intelligence. Lift your head up to where the answers are. That's how you'll able to access the intelligence."

Lucas did just as Miss Miller had instructed. He took a deep breath like he was going to stick his head under water, but instead, he thought about sticking his head into this imaginary cloud of intelligence. He stood a little straighter and taller. He raised his chin, looked up, smiled, and squeezed the crystal. Miss Miller spoke with such certainty about the intelligence that Lucas almost expected to see it. And then, to his amazement, Lucas saw tiny points of light, like tiny fireflies, darting around quickly just above his head.

"Wow!" said Lucas as he was looking up.

"What do you see?" asked Hailey.

"It's really cool! It's like a bunch of tiny stars bouncing around just above my head."

"Lucas, I think Hailey would like to see what you are seeing," said Mrs. Moore. "Hold out your hand and take Hailey's hand."

Hailey grabbed Lucas's hand, looked up and began to see the little stars bouncing around just above her head.

"Wow is right!" exclaimed Hailey. "This is amazing. It's so beautiful!"

When one speck of light shot in his direction, Lucas almost ducked his head, but decided to let it hit him to see what happened. It was almost as if his mind was getting brighter and his thoughts became clear. It was then he realized the investigator was not the problem. Lucas began smiling.

You're smiling," said Miss Miller. "What question or problem did you have? Did you find the answer? Would you like to share what you experienced?"

"Well, when Mallory told us a private investigator was looking into the disappearance of Senka, I began to worry what might happen if he started asking me questions. But just now, when I thought about the private investigator, I realized I had nothing to hide. I have no connection to Senka, other than the threats she made toward me and seeing her on the trail in Yosemite. Senka the wolf is not a problem I need to solve. She's gone."

"That's wonderful, Lucas!" exclaimed Mrs. Moore. "Did you learn anything else?"

"I have all of the solutions I need. Prescott has given me a Power Ring. I have friends and teachers all around me to help, teach and support me. I am one of the luckiest boys I know. If I have a problem, I have access to the best solution and I don't need to worry."

"That's a great attitude, Lucas," said Miss Harrison. "I believe you're starting to understand. Whatever you need, all that you have to do is ask, and it will come to you. It may take effort, thought and imagination. Intelligence may not come all at once or from the source you expect, but the answers will come. Well, that's all the time we have for today. Go home and practice what you have learned. Oh, and children, with all this excitement, don't forget to do the homework I assigned in class," she added with a wink.

Seven

Truth or Consequences

Before important decisions, consider the ripple effect of the consequences that could affect your future.

After class, Lucas walked Hailey home and then headed for his house. When he rounded the corner onto his street, he saw a shiny black truck parked in front of his house and wondered if someone was visiting. As he entered the house, he saw a tall man in the living room with his mom. He was perhaps fifty years old, and he looked like he might be a weightlifter. He still had most of his hair which was darker than his short graying beard.

"Lucas, this is Caleb Fairbanks," said his mother. "He's a private investigator who is looking into the disappearance of Mallory's aunt, and has some questions for you,"

The stranger reached out and shook his hand with a grip stronger than necessary.

"Hello Lucas. Your mother has been telling me some very interesting things."

Lucas thought back to the session with Mrs. Moore and how she had pulled out the dark feeling he had about Senka and replaced it with a calm feeling. He thought about how good he felt in the classroom. He stood up straight, smiled at Mr. Fairbanks, squeezed the crystal in his pocket and thought about all of the intelligence that was swirling around him and confidently asked, "How can I help you?"

"I understand you are friends with Mallory Fontaine," said Caleb.

"That's right, ever since she moved in across the street," replied Lucas.

Caleb handed Lucas a photograph of Senka. Lucas recognized the slender body and black hair with the white streak.

"Did you ever meet this woman?"

"Yes," replied Lucas.

There was no way he was going to say he first saw her in his dream while his family was camping. Lucas knew his mom had a good memory for names and faces and he was sure she would have remembered Senka from the trail in Yosemite.

"Where did you meet her?"

"I met her on the trail up to Vernal Falls in Yosemite."

"That's interesting," said Caleb. "Your mom said the same thing."

"Why is the truth so interesting?" asked Lucas.

"Because you told Mallory you had never met her aunt."

Lucas could see that the investigator was trying to cause some confusion to get him to make a mistake and say the wrong thing. With the intelligence power, Lucas was beginning to see things more clearly. He knew what the investigator was trying to do.

"When I saw Senka in Yosemite, I didn't know she was Malloy's aunt. I found out Senka was related to Mallory only after we came home from Yosemite."

"What about the ring?" asked Caleb.

"What ring are you talking about?" asked Lucas.

"Mallory said Senka had asked her to get a ring from you."

Lucas held up his hand and showed the investigator the silver and green ring on his finger and said, "You mean this one? I have a couple of rings like this. It's just a symbol to remind me to be honest. I had an extra ring and gave it to Mallory."

Caleb decided to try a different approach to catch Lucas in a lie or find a hole in his story.

"Your mother said you and your family went camping with Hailey's family near a ghost town last month. Do you know what we found between the ghost town and your campsite?" asked the investigator.

The power of intelligence was beginning to change the way Lucas thought about things, especially when the investigator began asking questions. Lucas noticed that his mind was being filled with thoughts and ideas.

"There are a lot of things to find in the desert. I've seen old rusted cars, bent horseshoes and a desert fox skeleton. I even found someone's wallet. But you're probably talking about the backpack Senka was wearing," replied Lucas.

Caleb was caught off guard and demanded, "How do you know about the backpack? The police haven't released that information. What do you know about the disappearance of Senka that you're not saying?"

"Just a minute!" said Hannah as she put her arm around Lucas. "I don't like the way you are talking to my son. He had nothing to do with her disappearance."

"There are some things that just don't add up," said Caleb without any apology. "The story I have from Mallory is that Senka was very interested in you Lucas, but you seem to know very little about her. I think you know more than you're telling me."

"I'm sorry Mallory's aunt is missing. I know Mallory loved her," said Lucas.

"I find it remarkable that Senka shows up when you're camping," said Caleb. "First she's in Yosemite and then in the desert near the ghost town. My years of investigative work have taught me there are no coincidences. Somehow you are connected to the disappearance of Senka, and I intend to find out how."

Lucas could see that his mom was ready to jump in and protect him, but he responded to the investigator before she could say anything.

"Mr. Fairbanks, I know about Senka's backpack near the ghost town because Mallory told me at school today," said Lucas calmly. "She also told me about the security video from the bus station and the mysterious man talking with Senka. Maybe you should find that man and ask *him* about Senka."

Lucas could see the investigator's face was starting to turn red and the veins in his temples were popping out. He probably did not like having a kid tell him how to do his work.

"Rather than focus on a ten-year-old boy from the neighborhood, maybe you'd get better results if you investigated the people who were seen with Senka," said Hannah sternly. "Have you considered that the man in the video at the bus station might be responsible for her disappearance?"

"We're already working on a lead for the man at the bus station," replied Caleb.

"Maybe Senka isn't who you think she is," said Lucas.

"Why would you say that?" asked Caleb.

"Mallory told me that although she loved her aunt, she also told me that sometimes Senka was not a very nice person," said Lucas.

"I don't think you are telling me everything you know young man," said Caleb harshly.

"And I think it's time for you to go Mr. Fairbanks," said Hannah as she stood up and pointed to the front door. The investigator knew he was no longer welcome and headed toward the door.

"Good day, Mrs. Lightfoot."

"Goodbye, Mr. Fairbanks!"

After the investigator left and the front door closed, Hannah turned to her son and asked, "What was that all about? It sounds like he's accusing you of something. It does seem odd that Senka was in Yosemite and again at the ghost town. Do you really know more about this?"

"Mom, Senka is not a nice person. First, she's not really Mallory's aunt. She was adopted by her uncle. Even Mallory says that sometimes Senka can be mean."

"Why would she want the ring on your finger?"

"She doesn't want this ring," said Lucas as he pointed to his hand. "She wants the Power Ring that Prescott gave me. She wants to use it for the power it has, but I don't believe she wanted to use it for good things. I think Senka had plans to use it for dark power."

"Lucas, you just said 'Senka *had* plans". Does she no longer have those plans or is she missing because she's dead?"

Lucas was now faced with a choice. To use the Power Ring correctly, he needed to have virtue and be honest. There were some details he had not told his parents. He never lied to them, but he didn't tell them all the facts either. His parents had met Prescott and Katrina and they now knew Grandpa Jack was a Light Bearer. Lucas was surprised they accepted all of this so calmly. Lucas's mom and dad had trusted him enough to let him continue training to be a Light Bearer and, Lucas decided, it was time to trust them with the truth about Senka regardless of the consequences.

"Mom, I said Senka was not a kind person, but there is more I need to tell you about what happened in the desert," said Lucas.

Lucas's mom could see her son was carrying a heavy burden and said, "I want you to know that you can tell me anything. I love you and will help you no matter what happened."

"Mom, I know this is going to sound strange and hard to believe, but the truth is, Senka had the ability to change into a wolf and back into a woman. She was trying to steal the Power Ring."

Hannah had a look of surprise and disbelief. She was not expecting to hear something quite so strange. She was silent for a moment as she thought about what her son had just revealed.

"You mean she's a werewolf?"

"I don't think so," replied Lucas. "She's the one who broke into our home and stole the Power Ring from my room. With help from Hailey and some parrots, I was able to get it back again. Senka, in her wolf form, found us in the desert when Hailey and I were riding back to camp on our quads during the thunderstorm. I knew Hailey and I were in danger, and I needed to do something to keep us safe. I was able to trick the wolf into coming into the middle of the riverbed at just the right time. I was hoping the water would carry her downstream. Instead, she was killed when the flash flood picked up my quad and it landed on top of the wolf's head. Hailey and I buried the wolf in the middle of the riverbed in the desert."

Lucas then told his mom about the encounter with Senka in Yosemite and how he saved Gavin by the lake with the help of the bears and hawks from the forest.

Hannah looked very surprised and asked, "Are you telling me that with the Power Ring, you can talk to animals?"

"Yes, Mom, I can."

She turned and stared out the sliding glass door. He thought her silence might be because she was trying to make sense of everything he had told her. Lucas wished he knew what was going on inside her head, but he did not have permission to listen to her thoughts. Maybe she was going to change her mind and stop him from training to be a Light Bearer. Maybe she was going to make him give the Power Ring back to Prescott or Grandpa Jack. Maybe she was going to give Prescott back to Katrina. Lucas thought his adventures were over. After a brief silence, his mother then turned to face Lucas. He saw tears welling up in her eyes and spilling down her cheeks.

"Thank you for telling me what happened and for being truthful."

Lucas was sure this was the end and wondered how he could possibly say goodbye to Prescott.

After a long silence, his mom said, "I'm so proud of you Lucas!" She wrapped her arms around him and gave him an extra-long hug. "You are so brave to save Gavin and Hailey. It seems I am learning more and more about my amazing son. You were very clever to outsmart the wolf. I can see why Prescott and your grandpa want you to become a Light Bearer. Lucas, I want you to be a Light Bearer too, but I also want you to be careful. I don't want you getting hurt."

With relief, Lucas replied, "I will Mom. I will be careful."

"Hey Mom – can I ask you something?"

"You can ask me anything, Lucas."

"Got any of those cookies you made yesterday? They were so good!"

They both laughed with relief to be able to talk about simple things.

"I do – and you can have as many as you like – with a big glass of milk!"

Eight

Shape Shifting

*We often know the truth in our hearts
before we know it in our minds.*

Miss Harrison walked into class a few minutes late with a blond-haired boy and girl following her. "Good morning class. I would like to introduce two new students to our class. This is Tanis Smith and her brother Damian. They just moved here from Arizona, and I would like you to welcome them to our school."

There were two empty desks in the last row near Hailey and Miss Harrison directed the two new students to sit in those seats. Hailey figured they must be twins since they were in the same class. When they sat down, Damian was next to Hailey and Tanis sat in front of her brother. They both turned to Hailey to introduce themselves.

"Hi, as you heard, my name is Damian, and this is my twin sister Tanis. What's your name?"

"I'm Hailey and these are my friends Lucas and Mallory."

Lucas and Mallory waved and just said hello. Hailey thought it was strange that after Lucas said hello, the twins looked at each other and grinned. She detected a slight nod of his head as Damian smiled at his sister. Miss Harrison brought the class to order and handed the class assignment to the front of each row and asked the students to take one and pass the others back.

"Let's begin class today with an exercise in multiplication word problems," said Miss Harrison.

There was an audible groan from some of the students.

"I'm ignoring your protests," said Miss Harrison with a smile. "You will have twenty minutes to answer the twenty questions. I would like you to show your calculations in the space beside the questions and put your answer in the box."

Miss Harrison set the timer on her phone and said, "All right, everyone, begin."

Hailey saw that it was 8:40 so they had to be done at 9:00. She concentrated on working out the math problems and was in the middle of the first page, when out of the corner of her left eye, she saw Damian and Tanis turn to the second page at the same time. Hailey thought this was strange but kept working.

She had just finished the first problem on the second page when the twins turned to page three at the same time. The speed at which the twins were solving the problems quickly went from being interesting to annoying. Not only were the twins cute, but they appeared to be smart. They finished the last question at the same time and turned their papers upside down and looked up at the clock.

Hailey glanced at the clock to see just how fast they were. It was 8:52. It had only taken them twelve minutes to finish the test. Hailey enjoyed being a straight-A student. She rarely bragged about how smart she was except when she was joking with Lucas. She had always been one of the smartest students in the class, but now she had serious competition. She struggled with the questions on the last page but finished with thirty seconds to spare.

"Okay. Times up," said Miss Harrison. "Pass your papers to the person next to you so we can grade them."

Hailey looked over at Damian and they exchanged papers. As Miss Harrison went through the answers, Hailey found that Damian answered every single question correctly which only added to her annoyance. When Hailey got her paper back from Damian, she saw she had missed only one question. Hailey took a quick glance at the score Tanis had on her test when it was handed back. She got all of them correct.

"I know some of you didn't finish and that's okay," said Miss Harrison. "This was meant to be tough so I can get a measure of your level of understating. Pass your papers forward please."

Damian turned to Hailey and said, "You did really well just by finishing the test. It sounds like most of the others didn't finish at all. The question you missed was very misleading and anyone could have made the mistake."

"Thanks," said Hailey. "But you and your sister finished early and got them all correct. How did you do that?"

"We went to a special school," replied Damian.

"What kind of school?"

"It was a school for gifted children in Surprise, Arizona near Phoenix," said Damian.

"Tanis is actually the intelligent one," admitted Damian. "I got in because she's smart and I'm her twin brother."

It was barely noticeable, but when she looked into Damian's eyes, Hailey thought she saw a flash of yellow in his eyes. Maybe it was the reflection of something outside, but a chill ran down her spine that forced her to pay attention to her feelings.

"Hailey," said Miss Harrison, "is there something you want to share with the class?"

"No, Miss Harrison." replied Hailey striking an attentive pose.

There was something different about Damian and Tanis, but it was more than just being smart or cute thought Hailey. She had learned to pay attention to her feelings. She often felt things in her heart that were not explained by her normal senses, and she knew she needed to talk with Lucas. Now that the test was over, Lucas and Hailey could share their thoughts again.

"Lucas, can you hear me?" asked Hailey in her mind.

"Sure," replied Lucas. *"What's up?"*

"When I was talking with Damian, I got a strange feeling," said Hailey. *"It was one of those sixth sense kinds of feelings. I think there's something dangerous about Damian and Tanis. I think they are hiding something."*

"Let's talk at lunch," said Lucas.

☼ ☼ ☼

Hailey and Lucas took their lunches to the far side of the field and sat on the grass under the trees behind Hailey's backyard. From that spot, they could see Mallory sitting at a table with Tanis and Damian.

"Something is not right with the twins," said Hailey. "The best way to describe the feeling,"

Hailey hesitated, "it's like I can feel it in my heart before I know why in my mind."

Lucas knew that Hailey had developed a strong, almost flawless sixth sense. When Hailey felt there was something wrong, Lucas had learned to listen to her. And, after all, Lucas and Hailey were both learning to trust their instincts and impressions.

"So, tell me what you think is unusual about them," said Lucas.

"The first thing I noticed was when we said hello to them. It was almost as if they already knew who we were. Then, when the math test was over, I saw that they both got perfect scores and they both finished the test at the same time in only twelve minutes."

"Maybe because they're twins, they have a natural mental telepathy and they were sharing the answers," suggested Lucas.

"I thought of that possibility, but they had to show their calculations," said Hailey. "It's more than that. I just think we should be careful around them."

☼ ☼ ☼

Tanis noticed that Lucas and Hailey had taken their lunch to the grass away from the school building and saw an opportunity to get to know their friend Mallory. In truth, the twins already knew a lot about her from Rebulus and saw her as a way to get the Power Ring.

During lunch, Tanis asked Mallory, "How well do you know Lucas and Hailey?"

"I live across the street from Lucas and the three of us have been friends since I moved here last year."

"But, how well do you really know them?" asked Tanis again.

"I don't know. I guess as well as any friends at school. We do homework together and hangout," replied Mallory. "Why are you asking?"

Tanis looked at Damian then back to Mallory and said, "We heard that your aunt is missing. Do you know where she is?"

Mallory was extremely surprised these new students from another state would know that her aunt was missing.

"What do you mean? How did you hear about my aunt?" questioned Mallory.

"We have a friend who knows your aunt. He told us that your friends Lucas and Hailey were in the desert the same time your aunt disappeared. He thinks maybe they can help find her," suggested Damian.

Damian was being devious, hoping to plant some negative thoughts in Mallory's mind to get her to turn against Lucas and Hailey. If he could work it right, Mallory might help them get the Power Ring. It had already been one week since they had been transformed into human form and they only had twenty-three days to finish their mission. Damian looked over at Hailey and Lucas, but they were not under the tree anymore. He looked all around the field expecting to see them walking back, but they seemed to have disappeared. Damian wanted to make sure no one was around to listen in on his conversation with Mallory.

"I heard that a private investigator talked with Lucas and his family about your aunt," said Damian. "Maybe he should talk with Hailey as well."

Mallory was confused by this whole conversation and thought it was odd that the twins knew about her aunt. She briefly wondered if she should trust them, but the chance that they could help clouded her judgement and replied, "Yes, maybe he should interview Hailey. Any information will be good. I'll talk with my uncle and suggest the investigator talk with Hailey."

"I think it would be better if you don't say anything to Hailey," advised Tanis. "It will be better not to warn her."

"Why not?" asked Mallory.

"Just in case she's hiding something, she won't have time to make up a false story," replied Tanis.

"Do you think Lucas and Hailey would lie about my aunt?" asked Mallory surprised.

"I think they would try to protect their secret," said Tanis.

"What secret are you talking about?" questioned Mallory, thinking this conversation wasn't making any sense at all.

"We don't know what it is, but our friend said they're hiding something," insisted Tanis. But Tanis did know their secret. She knew about the Power Ring that would soon be theirs. Tanis noticed that Damian kept looking around. He appeared nervous about something.

"What's wrong Damian? You keep looking around like someone is going to sneak up on you."

"I just want to make sure we keep this conversation private." replied Damian as he gave Mallory a look as if to say, 'don't breathe a word of this.'

The bell rang to end lunch. Mallory agreed the investigator should talk with Hailey. Damian was about to walk into class when he saw Lucas come around the corner of the building like he had been running. Damian was glad to see Lucas had not been near the lunch tables.

That afternoon, Miss Harrison had scheduled library time for ten of the students to research information for a report on one of the fifty states. She dismissed the students and directed the rest of the class to read from their assigned book. Lucas, Hailey, and Mallory were in the first group of students headed to the library. Mallory looked back over her shoulder at Tanis who put her finger to her lips indicating silence. A few minutes later, Mallory came back into the classroom and told Miss Harrison she forgot something at her desk. She picked up a folder from her desk and whispered to Tanis.

"Let's talk after school in the library."

Tanis nodded her head in agreement and Mallory turned and headed out the door.

☼ ☼ ☼

After school Mallory found Tanis and Damian in the library as planned.

"Do you have some new information?" asked Tanis.

"No, I just wanted you to tell me again what you said earlier during lunch, so I don't forget anything," replied Mallory.

Tanis and Damian looked at each other and wondered if Mallory was really so forgetful.

"You're supposed to have the private investigator interview Hailey so he can get her to slip up and tell what really happened in the desert."

"What do you think really happened in the desert?" asked Mallory.

"We can't tell you how we got the information, and you can't say any of this to the investigator, but we're sure both Lucas and Hailey are hiding something. They know more than they're telling about your aunt," assured Damian.

"Okay," said Mallory. "Leave it to me."

The three walked out of the library with the twins turning left and Mallory turning right. Mallory rounded the corner of the library and came face to face with Lucas.

Lucas looked right at Mallory and asked, "How did it go?"

Lucas watched as the copy of Mallory shifted back into Hailey who replied, "We have a serious problem!"

As they walked home, Hailey told Lucas everything she learned. Together, they came up with a plan to help Mallory and to figure out who the twins really were.

Nine

African Race of Life

*The eyes are useless if the heart
and the mind are blind*

Lucas and Hailey were excited about their tutoring session for today, which wasn't after school, but before school started. Katrina had planned to pick up Lucas and Hailey and go with them to Miss Harrison's classroom at seven in the morning. Katrina told the children she had other responsibilities, gave them hugs, wished them well, and left them at the classroom door. When they walked in, Miss Miller and Mrs. Moore, the empath, were waiting with Miss Harrison.

"Good morning, Hailey. Good morning, Lucas," greeted Mrs. Moore. "Thank you for coming early. We have a wonderful lesson planned for today. Do you have your passports ready?"

Lucas and Hailey both held up their arms to reveal the bracelets they had been given.

Hailey could not contain her excitement and asked, "Where are we going today?"

Mrs. Moore smiled and said, "We're going to the Kruger National Park to meet Michael Naidoo."

"Kruger National Park? Where's that?" asked Hailey.

"It's about 300 miles northeast of Johannesburg, South Africa," replied Miss Miller.

"Really! We're going to Africa?" asked Hailey excitedly.

"Remember, it will only be virtual travel, but your senses will think it's real. It's summertime there and we will arrive in the late afternoon which is why we asked you to come early. Michael Naidoo will be your guide and he's waiting for us."

"Miss Harrison will be here when you get back to the classroom," said Miss Miller.

"I'll see you when you return," said Miss Harrison with a gleam in her eye. "Enjoy your trip."

Miss Miller directed Hailey and Lucas to stand and face each other about three feet apart. Mrs. Moore and Miss Miller stood on either side of the children, the four of them forming a circle. Mrs. Moore reached into her bag and pulled out a blue crystal pyramid about the size of an egg and held it out in the center of the circle. She slowly withdrew her hand and the pyramid floated between Lucas and Hailey's eyes.

"Wow!" said Lucas. "How cool is that! Wait, how does it float in mid-air?"

"I'm sure they could explain the scientific reason it floats," said Hailey with a smile, "but I like to think that, maybe, it's just magic."

Lucas saw the teachers smile at each other, but they said nothing. Lucas realized the crystal pyramid floating in mid-air was quite ordinary when compared to some of the other magical things that have happened.

"Now, hold out your arm with your passport bracelet and put it in the center of the circle. Take hold of the person's wrist to your left, so our hands form a square in the center," said Mrs. Moore. "This will be a new and thrilling experience so remember to breathe. You will see white lights and hear the sound of rushing water. Remember, don't let go until we get to Africa!"

Hailey imagined flying to Africa and wondered if she let go would she fall into the ocean.

"What will happen if we let go?" asked Hailey.

Mrs. Moore could sense a sincere concern from Hailey and said, "There is no reason to worry. If you let go before we arrive, the travel stops and we're all back in the classroom. Are you ready?"

Lucas and Hailey nodded and reached out forming a square with the Master Light Bearers. As soon as they clasped hands to arms, Lucas and Hailey felt a small jolt of electricity as four narrow beams of blue light shot out of the crystal directly at the sun symbol on their passport bracelets. Hailey let out a short scream and grabbed Mrs. Moore's arm tighter. The classroom faded away and the only thing Lucas could see behind Hailey were moving points of white light. He heard a sound of rushing water, like a waterfall. A few seconds later the dancing white lights gave way to the golden light of the afternoon sun. Lucas and Hailey found themselves standing in a grassy field on a hill which sloped downward on three sides. They released the square grip and turned to look around. They were standing in tall grass up to their knees. The warm gentle breeze was dry with a slight aroma that reminded Lucas of animals at the zoo. But more than that, the breeze brought the scent of life itself. To the left about a quarter mile away was a grove of green trees and to the right was a slow-moving river.

"Hello Lucas and Hailey! Welcome to my beautiful country!"

They turned around to see the voice was from a young man in his thirties. His skin was dark, and his head shaved smooth. His eyes were a shimmering light blue which made for a remarkable appearance. Lucas could sense there was something special about him. Maybe he was on the Light Bearer Council.

"Welcome," he said again. "My name is Michael Danish Naidoo and it's such an honor to meet the new Light Bearers!"

Lucas expected to greet Michael with a handshake. Instead, Michael grabbed Lucas's hand and gave him a left-handed bear hug. Michael stepped toward Hailey and greeted her in similar fashion. He then turned to Miss Miller and Mrs. Moore who were standing side by side and he wrapped his arms around both and hugged tightly, which made them smile and look surprised.

Hailey asked Lucas in his mind, *"Did you feel something when Michael hugged you?*

"Oh yes, I did," replied Lucas. *"It felt very energizing like he was giving me power and strength."*

"I know, right?" replied Hailey. *"It's hard to explain, but I feel stronger."*

Michael turned his attention back to Lucas and Hailey.

"I would like to introduce you to my young friends," said Michael. "This is William Barrett and Mia Shigley. I have chosen William and Mia to be trained as a Light Bearers just as you have been chosen by someone on the council."

William looked to be a year or two older than Lucas. He was dark-skinned like Michael with short cropped black hair. He was wearing a long yellow shirt with a design around the neck, brown pants, and sandals. Mia was about Hailey's height and wore a sage green shirt and tan pants with high lace-up boots. Her wide-brim hat covered her brown hair and protected her fair skin. Hailey thought she looked out of place and wondered where she was from, that is, until she spoke.

"G'day and welcome to the bush," said Mia with a smile. "I'm stoked to meet ya."

The accent was unmistakable. Hailey immediately knew she was from Australia.

William raised his hand and said, "Hey guys. Good to meet you. Michael has something exciting planned for you."

"In Africa, our names are very important," said Michael. "My father named me Michael for the archangel who fought against the dragon and my mother named me Danish which means knowledge and wisdom. Naidoo is my family name which means patient. Lucas, Hailey, I have heard good things about both of you."

Lucas and Hailey looked at each other and wondered what had been said about them.

"Lucas, I know your name means a *quick messenger of light*," said Michael. "It's such a great name for a Light Bearer. It was almost as if your parents knew who you would become."

"Hailey, do you know what your name means?" asked Michael turning toward her.

She shook her head.

"Hailey comes from the Norse word for *heroine*. Sinclair has several meanings, but the one for you is *bright*."

"That makes you a shining hero!" said Lucas with a smile.

Hailey was always very observant of even the smallest of details. She had noticed that when Michael spoke with her, he wasn't looking at her but maybe beyond her to the horizon and wondered if Michael was blind. She started to ask but thought it might be rude.

Instead, she asked, "What... um... where are we?"

"This is Kruger National Park in South Africa," said Michael. "It is the oldest and I think the finest animal park in all of Africa. And Hailey, if you're wondering if I'm blind, I am."

"How did you know I was thinking that? Can you read my mind?"

"Of course not," replied Michael. "I have other ways to know what is going on in my world. There was a short hesitation in your voice and the tone of your voice changed slightly. I figured you were wondering about my blindness."

"How long have you been blind? If it's okay to ask," stammered Hailey.

"I have been blind since birth," replied Michael, "but I do not accept blindness as a handicap."

Michael turned to William and asked, "What am I always telling you about blindness?"

"The eyes are useless if the heart and the mind are blind. We look with our eyes, but we really see with our heart and mind," replied William.

Michael raised his hands above his head, clapped three times and let out a loud chirping sound.

"That's right! Even though I do not see with my eyes, I see so much more in other ways."

He pointed to the sky behind them. A large dark brown bird with a massive wingspan swooped down around them and landed on Michael's waiting arm. Lucas felt the gust of wind on his face as the majestic bird flapped its wings to land. It was then he noticed that Michael had put on a leather glove where the bird landed.

"Hailey and Lucas let me introduce you to Echo Hawk. She's an African Hawk-Eagle and, when I need to see, she is my sight."

Echo Hawk had dark brown feathers on her back and white and black feathers on her chest and wings. She was about eighteen inches tall with a hook in her beak that looked like most eagles Lucas had seen. She had piercing yellow eyes that closely watched the visitors who were with Michael. Lucas and Hailey had the same thought and turned their Power Rings to telepathy. Lucas was the first to speak.

"Hello Echo, my name is Lucas, and this is my friend Hailey."

Echo Hawk cocked her head with a questioning stare and then looked at Michael who nodded his head and said, "It's okay. You may show your true self."

Echo Hawk then flew to a large flat stone a few feet away and faced the visitors. She began spinning faster and faster until she was a blur to the onlookers. When she slowed her twirling and came to a stop, the hawk had transformed into a young woman. The breast feathers were replaced with a long brown leather tunic. She wore dark brown tights and tall

leather boots. The wings had disappeared and were replaced by her arms. When she raised her head, Lucas saw she still had the piercing yellow eyes of the hawk.

"Master Lucas and Milady Hailey," said Echo Hawk. "It is an honor to meet the new generation of Light Bearers."

Hailey replied, "We are thrilled to have been chosen and to learn from the masters."

Miss Miller saw that the children were enjoying the conversation with Echo, but she knew it was time to begin the lesson without delay.

"Hailey and Lucas, we have brought you here to introduce you to Michael. He is one of the seven members of the Light Bearer Council," said Miss Miller. "You will have an opportunity to meet with all of the council members and learn from them."

"Ahh! I knew it!" thought Lucas.

"Michael," said Mrs. Moore, "we will need to get Lucas and Hailey back to their class before school starts. Is there something you have for them?"

"Yes, yes. Come with me so we can get a better view of the river. Echo Hawk, I will need your eyes now."

"Of course," replied Echo and she quickly transformed back into an African Hawk-Eagle, beat her mighty wings to fly away and was soon floating over the river.

Lucas and Hailey followed Michael to a place where they could see a herd of animals with long curved horns drinking at the river. They were tan in color over most of their bodies with a black streak on the sides and a white under belly.

"What kind of animals are those?" asked Hailey. "They look like antelopes."

"They are gazelles, a member of the antelope family, but a little smaller. They can run fast and jump high. Sometimes they can even outrun a predator."

"Who are their predators?" asked Lucas.

"Let me tell you about life here in Africa. Every morning in Africa, a gazelle awakens. She wants to eat, but she has one thought she must keep foremost in her mind. She must be able to run faster than the fastest lion. If she cannot, then she will be eaten. Every morning in Africa a lion awakens. She is hungry and must feed her family. She has only one thought on her mind. She must be able to run faster than the slowest gazelle. If she cannot, she will die of hunger. Whether you choose to be a gazelle, or a lion is of no consequence. It is enough to know that with the rising of the sun, you must run. And you must run faster than you did yesterday, or you will die. This is the race of life."

"Do you want to show them what you mean?" asked Miss Miller.

"Yes of course," said Michael. "Lucas, I think you will be a great lion. Hailey, you will make a lovely and graceful gazelle."

"What do you mean?" asked Hailey. "I don't want to be eaten."

"Then you had better run faster than me," teased Lucas.

Michael reached out and grasped Lucas and Hailey by their hands and said, "Let us begin."

In an instant, Lucas realized he was looking through the eyes of a lion. He *was* the lion. He knew he was still Lucas in the lion's body, but he was experiencing the lion's instincts and muscled strength. The strongest thought he had was to feed his cubs. He seemed to move only on instinct, deeply focused on finding food.

At the same instant, Hailey found herself looking through the eyes of one of the gazelles drinking from the river. She was surrounded by other gazelles in the herd lapping cool water from the river. Hailey knew she was still herself but, at the same time felt a natural connection to the herd that made her feel safe and protected. Several of her sister gazelles had waded into the river to cover themselves with more of the cooling waters. Suddenly, Hailey's senses screamed danger. She looked up to see a crocodile lunge out of the water to attack another gazelle.

As if they were all linked together, the gazelles moved in unison and dashed away from the water to the safety of the trees and the grassland. What amazed Hailey was her ability to run and jump on four legs with such speed and agility. It felt so fluid, so swift – twenty times better than having the newest pair of running shoes!

Hailey looked back at the river and saw the crocodile still thrashing its powerful jaws back and forth until the gazelle lay still. Hailey knew none of this was real, or at least she thought she was still in the classroom at school, but every one of her senses convinced her to believe she was a gazelle in South Africa! Seeing the gazelle pulled under the water by the crocodile was not as sad as she thought it should be. It was just the way of life for animals in Africa.

Lucas crept slowly toward the herd of gazelles. Somehow, he knew, with the breeze blowing toward him, the gazelles would not catch his scent and he had a better chance of finding dinner for his pride. He looked beyond the herd and saw a cheetah approaching from the other side. Lucas thought how wonderful for his family that the gazelles would catch the scent of the cheetah, turn as one, and run straight toward his waiting claws. Even as Lucas was wondering if a lion would really have those thoughts, that was exactly what happened.

As the gazelles ran toward him, he locked his gaze on one particularly beautiful and graceful gazelle and wondered if it was Hailey. The natural impulse of the lion took over and Lucas sprang forward with his powerful legs and gave chase. He was keenly aware how driven he was by instinct to chase the gazelles. Lucas was amazed to feel the powerful muscles in his legs pushing him faster than he had ever ridden on his quad in the desert.

Hailey could not remember a time when she was so frightened. She ran with the herd away from the cheetah only to be surprised by the lion. Every time Hailey darted one way the swift lion followed. She was surprised that the powerful lion was so nimble and wondered if it was really Lucas. She wanted to stop and scream at the lion to stop chasing her, but a survival instinct forced her to keep running.

So, this was the race of life Michael described for them. Several other gazelles were right next to her, all racing for their lives. The lion was so close she could hear his panting. She was running beside two sister gazelles and sometimes they would bump into each other, which added to the confusion of which way to turn to escape the beast following them.

This chase went on for several minutes and she was exhausted. How could she survive? One of her sisters darted to the right and ran back toward the safety of the herd. It was just two of them now and if she could be faster or smarter

than her sister, she just might stay alive one more day. Hailey and the other gazelle were now running in a dry creek with banks on both sides. Running over the rocks and stones was difficult and she was slowing down. The only way to save herself from the deadly claws of the lion was to jump up and over the bank. She saw a slight rise in front of her that would give her a springboard to get to the top of the bank. Her only hope now was to jump higher than the lion. She used the last measure of her remaining strength to increase her speed and hit the rise as fast as possible. She leapt with all her ability to the top of the bank. One of her back legs missed the edge but, with determination, she hooked her front legs over a tree root and scrambled over the edge of the bank. Hailey quickly looked back as she continued to run and saw the lion chasing and capturing her sister gazelle with his powerful claws and bringing the gazelle down in a cloud of dust.

As quickly as the visual experience had started, it ended with a sharp snapping sound like the crack of a whip. Lucas and Hailey were back on the hill looking over the river with the gazelles. Off to the left they saw the lion with the lifeless gazelle, now surrounded by the hungry cubs.

"Welcome back!" said Michael. "How was your experience as the lion and the gazelle? What did you learn?"

Lucas could still feel his heart pounding hard and his hands were shaking from the excitement of chasing the gazelle. Hailey felt like she had just finished running a marathon and was still trying to catch her breath.

"I need to run... faster!" said Hailey between breaths.

"How did you get away from the lion?" asked Michael.

"I looked for a place to go," wheezed Hailey as she paused to breathe, "....where I could out jump the lion. I knew I needed to go where the lion could not. I kind of feel sorry for the other gazelle though."

"Lucas, it appears the gazelle you were chasing outsmarted you. How did you catch the other gazelle?" asked Michael smiling.

"I was watching the gazelles running from me. I lost the first one because her movements were changing, and she was unpredictable. The other two gazelles had a rhythm as they ran together, and I knew which way they would turn. I just moved to the place where the gazelles were going to be. Hailey, I'm sorry. I didn't know you were the gazelle I was chasing. It wasn't me trying to kill you. It was just the instinct of the lion."

"I know," nodded Hailey. "I know it was the lion and not you."

"I hope that being the lion and the gazelle has opened your eyes to a new understanding," said Michael. "Whether you are a lion, a gazelle, or a young Light Bearer, you must look for ways to outsmart your enemy and escape. You need to anticipate the enemy's every move. Lucas, the strong desire you felt to chase the gazelle is no different than the fierce desire your enemy might feel to chase you. Hailey, the passion you felt to stay alive is what you need to outsmart your enemy."

"This is one experience I will never forget," said Lucas. Hailey nodded her head in agreement.

"I would like to give you one more thing to keep as a way to remember this adventure," said Michael as he handed Lucas and Hailey a gold coin the size of a half dollar to each of them.

One side of the coin had a picture of a gazelle and a lion standing tall side by side with a square hole in the center of the coin. They turned the coin over and saw some words raised on the surface and read along as Michael read the words to them.

"You are smart. You are strong. You are brave. Belief will make it so."

"It's time to go back to the classroom," said Miss Miller. "Thank you, Michael."

"This was so real I forgot we were not really in Africa," said Hailey.

"Lucas and Hailey, it was an honor to meet you," said William. "I hope we meet again."

"I'm sure we will," said Lucas. "The Light Bearers need to stick together."

"Be safe," exclaimed Mia. "It was so good to meet 'cha.'"

Michael came over to Lucas and Hailey and gave them each a hug that rippled energy through their being and said, "Safe travels my friends. Maybe the next time we meet, it will be in your city where there's a gathering of Light Bearers. Oh, and keep these coins with you. They will be a key needed to unlock a mystery in your future."

The children exchanged glances and carefully pocketed their coins.

Miss Miller and Mrs. Moore positioned Lucas and Hailey in the circle again with the blue pyramid crystal floating in the center. Suddenly, the grasslands of Africa disappeared in the brilliance of a white light. When the light faded, they were back in their classroom. Lucas and Hailey were facing each other but Miss Miller and Mrs. Moore were gone.

"Welcome back to school," said Miss Harrison with a smile.

"What happened to Miss Miller and Mrs. Moore?" asked Hailey

"They are both teachers like me and had to go prepare their own classrooms for school this morning. I trust that Michael's outdoor classroom gave you a chance to learn in a new and different way."

"It was not like any classroom I've ever been in before," said Hailey shaking her head with amazement.

"Tomorrow we will journey to visit other Master Light Bearers," said Miss Harrison. "Katrina will arrange to bring you to school early in the morning again so get plenty of rest tonight."

☼ ☼ ☼

Later that day, as Lucas and Hailey were walking home from school, Lucas put his hand in his pocket and felt something he didn't remember having. He pulled out the gold coin Michael had given to him. Hailey had a confused look as she pulled a coin from her pocket.

"Lucas, we were in the classroom the whole time, right?"

"I think so. It was just a virtual travel to Africa we experienced. It was only in our minds, right?"

"If we were not really in Africa, how did these coins from Michael get into our pockets?" asked Hailey.

"I don't know" said Lucas with a smile. "It must be magic."

And they both giggled.

Ten

English Statues

What you think, what you see and what you do, you will become.

Arrangements had been made for the visit and Katrina brought Lucas and Hailey to their classroom a few minutes before seven. The three teachers were already there.

"Where are we going today?" asked Hailey excitedly. "I hope it is not as dangerous as Africa."

"It should be less dangerous today. We're going to England," replied Mrs. Moore.

"Who are we going to meet in England," asked Lucas.

"The first person is Liam Kincaid. He's the leader of the Light Bearer Council," said Miss Miller, "He is certainly eager to meet with both of you."

Lucas, Hailey, Miss Miller, and Mrs. Moore stood in the circle as before and Mrs. Moore pulled out the blue crystal and let it float in the center of their circle. The same bright light appeared, and the sound of rushing water filled their ears. When the light faded, they were standing in what looked like a park surrounded by buildings. In front of them, they saw a very distinguished looking gentleman wearing a tailored brown suit. He had a full head of gray hair and a beard to match. The lines in his forehead and the wrinkles around his eyes suggested he was much older than Grandpa Jack. Lucas wondered what challenges Liam Kincaid might have faced to become the leader of the Light Bearer council and what his eyes had seen. Like other Light Bearers, and despite his age, he too had a glow surrounding him.

"Lucas and Hailey, I would like to introduce you to Liam 'Camelback' Kincaid," said Miss Miller.

He had a broad smile as he stepped toward to Lucas and Hailey and held out both of his hands. They each extended their hands to Liam Kincaid, and he held them together for a moment. A moment was all it took. Lucas and Hailey felt a soft jolt of electricity flow through their arms and into their bodies that felt the same as when Michael had hugged them in Africa. Lucas thought it was more than someone transferring power to him. It was like light energy flowing into him.

"Welcome my young friends. I'm so pleased to meet you. You must know how special you are to have been selected by a member of the council to be trained in the ways of the Light Bearers. Let me introduce you to a special lassie and my trainee, Megan Demeter."

Megan, who appeared to be about the same age as Lucas and Hailey, had a slender build with dark red hair and bangs cut just above her eyes. She wore a green dress with black tights and shiny black shoes. She had a playful grin and a twinkle in her eyes when she smiled.

"Delighted to meet you and welcome to London," said Megan as she did a slight curtsy. "I am happy to see more Light Bearers my age.

"It's great to meet you as well," said Hailey. "I love your accent. Are you from Ireland?"

"Aye. I was born in Dublin," replied Megan.

"It's really good to meet you and see we're not alone," said Lucas as he shook hands with Megan.

Megan then shook hands with Hailey and got close enough to whisper something into Hailey's ear. Hailey smiled and nodded in agreement.

"Hey, no secrets here," protested Lucas.

The girls looked at him, then at each other and giggled. Lucas was wondering what Megan had said to Hailey when Liam got everyone's attention.

"Come, walk with me," invited Liam. "There are some people I would like you to meet."

He pulled Lucas close to his right side and Hailey and Megan walked together on his left side as they started along a path in the park.

"Mr. Kincaid, where are we?" asked Hailey.

"We are in Belgrave Square Garden not far from Buckingham Palace," said Liam. "I would like to show you a statue of someone famous."

They stopped in front of a statue of a man sitting in a chair. The statue rested on a stone base engraved with the name "Christopher Columbus."

"I'm sure you know of Christopher Columbus," said Liam. "Like Columbus, you too are about to embark on a life-changing journey as a Light Bearer."

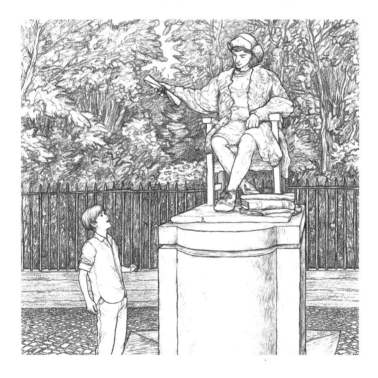

The statue of Columbus had a map rolled up in his right hand. He was looking off in the distance and was pointing with the map. Like Columbus, Lucas wondered what adventures awaited him. Every so often, Lucas had brief flashes of images he could see in his mind's eye. It occurred to Lucas, when Columbus crossed the uncharted ocean, he didn't have a map. Columbus created his own map. Using the stars to navigate, he was guided by his faith and a dream of finding a shorter route to India. Instead, he found a new land that changed the history of the world forever.

As he looked at the statue of Columbus, Lucas wondered aloud, "How did you have the courage to sail across the ocean in those tiny ships?"

Lucas was surprised when Columbus looked down and nodded to Lucas with a smile and spoke to him.

"Lucas Lightfoot, my courage was based on my knowledge of sailing and faith that I would reach my destination. I always felt, that for some reason, I was guided by some higher power. Your path will not always be clear or even known. Create your own map and move forward in faith. Someday, you too, may change the world."

Lucas turned to ask the others if they heard the statue talking, but they were already walking away. The teachers were talking with Liam and the girls were giggling in their own conversation. He looked back at Columbus. The statue had returned to its original position. Lucas shook his head. Maybe it was just his imagination. But, maybe, with a little magical help, Columbus was trying to guide him on his uncharted journey to become a Light Bearer.

Liam Kincaid turned and called out to Lucas. "Come Lucas, let's walk together and I'll tell you a story."

Lucas ran to catch up with the group and took his place on Liam's right side.

"This is a story told to me by my grandfather who lived in a small town south of Glasgow, Scotland. There is a legend of a king whose son was born with a hunch back, caused by a deformed spine that kept him from standing up straight. The king and queen adored their son and always treated the young prince with love and kindness. When the boy turned eight years old, his father asked him what he wanted for his birthday. The prince thought about it for several days, then told his father he wanted a statue of himself. The king was baffled as to why his son would want such a thing. The last thing in the world he wanted for his young son was for him to be mocked. In an effort to change the boy's mind, the king said, 'Surely there must be something else you desire.' The prince was steadfast. The prince turned his head to look up at his father from the bent position that limited his life. 'No, Father, there is nothing else. I want a statue of myself, but not as I appear now. Rather, I would like a statue of how I would look if I stood straight! I would like to have this statue placed in the garden outside my window where I can see it every day.'

"The king, though surprised by the request, ordered his best sculptor to carve the statue using the finest marble. When the statue was completed, the hunchback boy stood before his likeness each morning. Day after day he stretched and strained to mimic the six-foot replica of himself. He did this without fail for ten years. By his eighteenth birthday he stood tall, shoulders back, head straight, staring eye to eye with the beautiful marble statue. What was the prince's secret? It is this: What he thought and what he saw, he became."

"So, the statue became a goal for the young prince to reach," remarked Hailey thoughtfully.

"Exactly!" said Liam. "Many in the world see things as they are and think that's all there is. Wise are those who can see life not just as it is now but focus on what it can be tomorrow."

Liam let that thought sink into their minds as they walked in silence for a while. Lucas and Hailey were enjoying the sights of London and pointed to the funny, old fashioned looking black taxis and the red double-decker buses.

After walking a few blocks, they came to large stone archway. Hailey looked behind her to see if the teachers were still following them. When she turned around, she saw a lady walking a dog directly in front of her. Hailey stopped so she would not run into her, but the woman did not move aside. Hailey quickly put up her hands to protect herself and was surprised as the woman walked right through her. That's when she remembered this was a virtual trip.

Hailey turned around and saw the same woman walk through Mrs. Moore who just smiled at Hailey.

As they approached the archway, Mrs. Moore said, "This is Wellington Arch, honoring the victory of the Duke of Wellington over Napoleon. The statue on top is the Angel of Peace descending in a war chariot pulled by four horses."

Lucas was beginning to look for the meaning in everything he and Hailey saw and asked, "Does the statue mean that war comes before peace?"

"It is certainly one possible meaning," said Liam.

Several minutes later they were walking down a tree-lined path between a park and a road.

"Mr. Kincaid," began Hailey timidly, "I hope I am not being too rude, but where did you get the name Camelback?"

"You are not being rude at all, Hailey. My name is often the topic of discussion. I got the nickname of 'Camelback' many years ago. The story of the prince with the hunchback is my story. I too was born with a hunchback, and I had a hump like a camel. My wise father built a statue for me as well. He knew that I would one day become a Light Bearer. Although it took years to overcome and straighten out my back, the power of being a Light Bearer gave me the faith to never give up."

It was hard for Lucas to imagine Liam Kincaid with a hunchback. Lucas wondered if he would have had the courage and determination to do what Liam Kincaid had done to overcome his deformed back.

"This story is also your story Lucas. And yours as well, Hailey." said Liam.

"What do you mean?" asked Lucas.

"We all have some deformities or problems in our life, but they are not always visible or even physical," said Liam.

"You mean like having a heart defect?" asked Hailey. "It's on the inside but we can't see the defect."

"Yes, Hailey," said Liam. "Someone might have a heart defect and it's not obvious until they are involved in a physical activity that limits what they can do."

"There are other types of heart defects that are not physical," said Liam.

"How could a heart defect not be physical?" asked Lucas.

"Someone who has anger or hatred or jealously in their heart is what I would consider a heart defect," explained Liam. "People with these types of emotional defects limit how well they get along with other people and can be even more dangerous than a physical defect."

They came to the end of the park and the area opened to a huge building on their right. It was an impressive gray stone building three-stories high with a ten-foot-high fence made with black and gold bars.

"What's this building?" asked Hailey in awe.

"This is Buckingham Palace," replied Megan with pride. "It's where the Queen of England lives when she's in London. The queen and her family are referred to as royalty."

Liam stopped abruptly and got down on one knee so he could face the children eye to eye. "Listen carefully. All three of you are Light Bearers and that's all the royalty anyone needs."

Lucas was surprised by the thought that flashed in his mind. Is it possible Liam Kincaid was kneeling to royalty right there on the sidewalk in front of the palace?

"Lucas, I know both of your grandfathers," said Liam. "They are great Light Bearers and because of them, you have the birthright. There are many who have faith in you and your ability to bring light into the darkness. But you must develop the faith within yourself."

"What do you mean? How will I bring light into the darkness?" asked Lucas.

"You must continue your training to find the answer to that question," replied Liam. "I must go now. There is someone else you must meet."

"It's time to say goodbye to Mr. Kincaid and Megan and visit our second Master Light Bearer in England," said Miss Miler.

Lucas, Hailey, and the teachers said their goodbyes to Liam Kincaid and Megan. They turned and walked away but stopped. Liam handed something to Megan, and she ran back to Lucas and Hailey, held out her hands and said, "Mr. Kincaid asked me to give these to you and to tell you to keep them safe."

"What are they?" asked Hailey.

"He said they are part of the key, and you'll know what to do with them at the right time."

Megan gave Hailey a hug and whispered in her ear, "I heard who you are going to visit next, and I think he's off his trolley. Please, be safe! He's daft, that one!" Lucas was close enough to hear the warning to Hailey but didn't quite understand her meaning.

Megan turned to Lucas and smiled, "Cheers," then skipped away to catch up with Liam.

Lucas and Hailey looked at the gold pieces in their hands that were made in the shape of a lightning bolt. They were about two inches long and the wide end of the lightning bolt had a hole with a chain.

"What are we supposed to do with these?" asked Lucas.

"Put the chain around your neck and keep them safe," replied Miss Miller.

"Come. We have one more statue to see before we leave," said Mrs. Moore.

They walked around in front of Buckingham Palace and up the steps to a raised statue. They stood in the shadow of the afternoon sun looking up at a monument to Queen Victoria, their eyes drawn to the golden angel sitting on top of the monument.

"There sure are a lot of statues here in London," said Hailey. "We hardly ever see any statues where we live."

"Well, we do have a statue of Walt Disney and Mickey Mouse at Disneyland," said Mrs. Moore with a smile.

"The history of England is much older than where we live. Statues were created for hundreds of years to honor important people and special events in history," explained Miss Miller.

As Lucas and Hailey looked at the stone carving of the queen sitting on her throne, they both heard a voice in distinctive British accent.

"Children, I am so happy to see you."

They looked around, but the only people nearby were their teachers, and it was not their voices they heard. They looked up again at the statue of Queen Victoria and, to their surprise, she turned her head, looked down at them and smiled.

"I am happy to see you. Thank you for visiting me," said the statue in a soft voice.

Hailey whispered to Lucas, "Do you see what I see?"

"I do. Remember this is a virtual trip and none of this is real," whispered Lucas.

Again, the statue spoke. "Lucas and Hailey, I am very real. I served as Queen of the United Kingdom of Great Britain and Ireland for sixty-three years. I saw many changes in my lifetime. Because of my royal birthright, there were certain expectations and responsibilities that were required of me."

Lucas and Hailey stood amazed and speechless as the statue spoke with them.

"Lucas, you also have the birthright. Your legacy is that of a Light Bearer. Hailey, you have also been chosen to be a Light Bearer and to be an ally and support Lucas. Both of you are no less royal than any King or Queen of England. I was called to walk the path of a queen. You are called to walk the path of a Light Bearer and you must walk the path with honor."

"Where do I find the path of a Light Bearer?" asked Lucas.

"Each Light Bearer will have a different path, but all lead to the same destiny," replied Queen Victoria. "Your path will be defined by the choices you make each day. But there is also a path inside that your heart must journey. Each of us has a higher purpose. Yours has yet to be revealed. Lucas and Hailey, remember all you ever need is inside. Do not be afraid to look there."

The queen smiled at Lucas and Hailey then turned her head to the right and returned to her frozen-in-stone position.

"Time to go," declared Miss Miller. "We have one more Master to visit in England."

"Wait!" exclaimed Lucas. "Did you just see what we saw? Did you see the statue of Queen Victoria talking with us?"

"Of course, we did. We saw and heard everything," said Mrs. Moore. "We came here because she requested to speak with you. Did you gain any new understanding?

"We are to walk the path of Light Bearers and we are royalty like her," replied Lucas.

"It's important we choose the correct path and follow it with honor," added Hailey.

"Then you heard correctly," said Miss Miller. "Let's continue our travels. We have another Master Light Bearer to visit."

Eleven

Fallen Stones

When the head and the heart disagree, always choose the heart.

They formed a circle behind the statue of Queen Victoria and Mrs. Moore pulled out the blue crystal. The four travelers were soon enveloped in a ball of light once more. When the light faded, they were standing in an open field of green grass with large rectangular stones all around. Some stones were standing, and others were lying flat on the ground. There were low hills in the surrounding area. The sky was much darker than in London. The wind-driven clouds approaching them held the promise of thunder and lightning.

Thinking he was halfway around the world, Lucas was surprised to hear Prescott in his head. *"Be careful Lucas. Things are not always as they appear. Use the ring's power of intelligence to help you."*

Lucas was looking at the stones and concentrating on the warning from Prescott when Hailey snapped Lucas out of his thoughts with her bubbling enthusiasm.

"I know where we are," said Hailey excitedly. "This is Stonehenge."

"That's right," said a voice from behind.

Lucas turned around to see a tall bald-headed man with eyebrows that resembled fuzzy black and white caterpillars. He had a very thick gray mustache that extended from his nose back to his ears. The moustache resembled gray shredded wheat cereal.

"Good afternoon, Poppets. My name is Alastair Janus, and this is my young apprentice, Aiden Chong."

Aiden, who stood behind and a little to the side of Alastair, greeted Lucas and Hailey with a nod and said, "Hiya."

Alastair reached out and took Hailey's hand briefly. He then reached to greet Lucas. When Alastair shook hands with Lucas, the feeling was very different from the other Light Bearers. Lucas felt darkness or something threatening. But how could that be? Alastair was a Master Light Bearer and a member of the Council. Lucas had heard some strange things about Stonehenge and maybe that was the reason for the strange greeting from Mr. Janus. Or maybe it was just the dark and overcast sky surrounding them.

Lucas had been taught that when you speak with someone it was important to look them in the eye, but it was almost impossible not to stare at Alastair's mustache. The more he stared, the more he realized that much of Alastair's mustache was actually very long nose hairs combed into his mustache! He tried very hard not to giggle as he turned to look at Hailey. From the look on her face, Hailey had seen the "nose-stache" as well.

"I invited you here because I love this place," said Alastair heartily. "It's full of mystery and the unknown. Some of these stone are standing and others have fallen. Like stones, some people stand tall, and others will fall. Sometimes when things seem to be falling apart, they may actually be falling into place."

"What do you mean?" asked Lucas.

"Life is like a game of chess. To win you must make a move. Sometimes it's necessary to sacrifice a few chess pieces to win the game. Those who know the right moves are the ones who will be left standing. Knowing the right moves comes by learning, from experience and listening. When someone speaks to you, listen for what they say. But, more importantly, listen for what *isn't* being said."

"Mr. Janus, should we be listening for what you're not saying right now?" asked Hailey.

"Blimey, aren't you are the smart one," replied Alastair as he gave Hailey a sideways glance.

His gaze made her very uncomfortable as if he was trying to read her mind. Hailey thought it was a reasonable question, but his look gave her chills. But maybe it was just the wind.

Alastair turned to Miss Miller and said, "I like this little poppet. She is a bright one. Where did you find her?"

Miss Miller turned to look at Mrs. Moore then back at Alastair. "Hailey was chosen by Katrina and Prescott."

"Oh, right. That little lizard Prescott - is he still around?" questioned Alastair. Before she could answer, Alastair jumped back to Hailey's question.

"Yes, little Poppet, you should be listening for what is not being said. There will always be more than one way to look at a situation. People will say one thing and mean another. Listen to what people are saying and then listen for the true meaning and intent. Be careful and don't be fooled," he cautioned.

"We have a book at home on mythology and I remember Janus is the two-faced Roman god," said Lucas. No sooner had the words escaped his mouth, he regretted the way it sounded.

"You are correct, young squire. Janus was the Roman God of doorways or transitions. He is usually pictured with two faces, with each face looking in different directions. My family name is Janus, and I grew up with the belief that we always look at both sides of a story and to listen for what is *not* being said."

"How do we listen for what's *not* being said?" questioned Lucas.

"Think about what the other person wants most from you, not what they say they want," replied Alastair.

Lucas could not stop thinking about how he felt when shaking hands with Mr. Janus. Although Alastair Janus was a Master Light Bearer, something did not feel right.

"What do you want?" asked Lucas.

Alastair gave Lucas a long and cold stare, but then changed to an upbeat tone.

"Some of the Light Bearers on the council are getting old and need to retire. I want you to learn to be a Master Light Bearer and take your place on the Council with Hailey, Aiden, and others. It will become your responsibility to teach others," replied Alastair deliberately.

Lucas was beginning to understand the power of intelligence as brief flashes of inspiration entered his mind. What Lucas was sensing was different from what Mr. Janus was saying. He had a strong impression Alastair Janus really wanted to be the leader of the Council and take control over all Light Bearers.

In the short time they had been at Stonehenge, a cold wind started blowing from the East and menacing rain clouds gathered above them. Suddenly, a lightning bolt struck the earth very close with a blinding light. Lucas felt himself being pushed by the explosive sound from the thunder. He looked up at the stone behind Hailey as it began tottering toward her.

"Look out!" yelled Lucas as he ran and pushed Hailey out of the way. They both fell to the ground as the huge stone slammed into the earth just inches from Lucas's foot. The teachers ran over to help Lucas and Hailey.

"Are you alright?" asked Mrs. Moore.

"I think so," said Hailey.

"Yeah, I'm okay too," said Lucas as the teachers helped them to their feet.

"That was scary! That seemed all too real for a virtual trip," exclaimed Hailey as she reached to touch the stone. The stone felt hard and cold to her touch. It really appeared to be solid rock and Hailey wondered about the fine line between virtual reality and actual reality.

"If you have nothing further Mr. Janus, I believe this would be a good time to take our leave," said Miss Miller as she glared at Alastair.

"In just a moment, I have one final piece of advice for our young ones," insisted Alastair.

Lucas looked at Alastair who was standing on the other side of the fallen stone. He acted as if huge stones fall every day, and this was no big deal.

"When playing a game with someone, whether for fun or playing for keeps, watch yourself as closely as you watch your opponent. If he beats you, don't get upset or angry. That will interfere with your ability to learn. Instead, be thankful for the opportunity to learn from the situation. Study what the opponent did to win and determine how you will avoid mistakes in the future."

"Until we meet again," said Alastair as he stepped backward. He put his hand on Aiden's shoulder and nodded his farewell to the travelers. Alastair and Aiden then just simply disappeared.

"Well, that was interesting," said Mrs. Moore. But everyone knew she really meant 'that was really strange'.

"Thanks for saving my life, again," said Hailey.

"You're welcome," said Lucas. "I need to keep you around so you can return the favor someday."

"I think that's enough education for one day," said Miss Miller. "Let's go home."

Back in the classroom, Mrs. Moore asked, "Lucas, I sense there's some confusion in your mind."

"There is," replied Lucas. "The other Master Light Bearers we met had important lessons to teach us, but Mr. Janus didn't seem like he really wanted to help us. It felt more like a warning."

"Lucas, if I understand you correctly, your head and your heart don't agree with one another," said Mrs. Moore.

"That's it exactly," exclaimed Lucas.

"Your understanding of Alastair is probably close to the truth. I felt the same thing," assured Mrs. Moore. "Let me share with both of you a belief that guides my life. When the head and the heart disagree, always choose the heart. Your heart is the part of you that is most interested in your well-being."

Twelve

The Vanishing Wolf

*Change the way you look at the world
and your world will change.*

Lucas asked Mrs. Moore if he and Hailey could use the blue crystal to travel back to the desert to make sure the wolf was still buried under the rocks. He was concerned that maybe somehow the wolf had changed back to Senka, Mallory's aunt. If they found only the remains of the wolf, Lucas could relax and not worry about the investigator. But if they found something else, Lucas shuddered at the thought. Mrs. Moore agreed and met Lucas and Hailey in the classroom after school.

"Let me explain how the passports work," said Mrs. Moore. "You must both have a clear picture in your mind of where you want to go and hold fast to that picture when the crystal floats in front of you. Do you both remember exactly where you were and what it looked like?"

"The location is burned into my memory like I was there yesterday," replied Lucas. "Looking up the canyon behind the wolf, I could see the shadows in the hillside that looked like dark eyes looking at us. It was kind of spooky."

"And there was a small tree behind the wolf," said Hailey. "There were also some thorny shrubs on the left side of the riverbed."

"Can both of you think of the same place?" asked Mrs. Moore.

"I'm sure we can," said Lucas. "Let's stand looking north facing the water tomb where we piled the rocks on top of the wolf." He preferred to think of Senka as the wolf rather than as a human. It helped him get over Senka's death.

"Agreed," said Hailey.

Mrs. Moore did not need to rely on her empathetic gift to know that Lucas and Hailey were both excited and scared to go on this virtual trip. The nervous grins on their faces gave it away. The three of them clasped arms in a triangle this time and Mrs. Moore let the blue crystal float in the center. As always, these virtual trips brought the swirling white lights and the sound of water crashing in a waterfall.

Lucas and Hailey were glad to have the power of mental telepathy where they could not only talk to each other but share the same mental image of where they wanted to go. As the bright light faded, the trio found themselves in the riverbed. They were surprised to find that it was no longer dry. They were now standing in about six inches of water from the recent rains.

"Oh no!" exclaimed Hailey. "These are brand new shoes and now they're soaking wet!"

"This was a concern I had," said Mrs. Moore. "You knew where we were going, but unlike other trips we've made, there was no one at the destination to tell us what to expect."

"I hadn't thought about that," said Lucas.

"Don't worry," assured Mrs. Moore laughing. "Remember, this is just a virtual experience. When we get back our shoes will be dry."

They recognized the pile of rocks in front of them although it seemed smaller than before. Maybe the water had moved some of the rocks and sand thought Lucas.

"How do we find out if the wolf is still under the rocks?" asked Hailey.

"I'll take care of changing the direction of the water while you two lift the rocks and move the sand," suggested Mrs. Moore

The children nodded in agreement. Lucas watched as Mrs. Moore concentrated on the water. Amazingly, the water was divided into two streams that began to flow around the rocks as if there was an invisible barrier around the rock pile.

Lucas and Hailey used their telekinetic power to move the softball-size rocks, but the rocks kept bumping into each another.

"How about if you move the rocks on the right and I will move the rocks on the left," suggested Hailey.

That worked well until they got down to the last rock. The rock went straight up but started bouncing from side to side as if it was being hit by large invisible ping pong paddles. The large rock was about five feet in the air when it started vibrating violently. At the exact moment Hailey realized they were both trying to lift the same rock, it spilt loudly into two halves.

"Wow! Did you see that?" exclaimed Lucas.

"We were trying to move the same rock," said Hailey.

"I know, but did you see what we can do if we team up using our telekinetic power? It's kind of scary cool."

"Obviously there could be some serious consequences if you're not cautious when using your powers," said Mrs. Moore. "But you can also see how you have a way to protect yourselves if needed."

There was now just a small mound of sand in the middle of the riverbed. Lucas used the power of telekinesis to create a small sand volcano. The sand and pebbles in the riverbed began to bubble up, flow out from the center of the mound and spread outward in all directions making a six-foot diameter hole about four feet deep.

"I'm sure if the wolf bones were there, we would have seen them," said Hailey.

There was simply no evidence of the wolf ever being there. Mrs. Moore could feel the anxiety Lucas and Hailey were feeling.

"Are you sure this is the place?" asked Mrs. Moore.

Lucas looked over his shoulder at the tree they had clung to during the flash flood.

"There's the bolder we hid behind," said Lucas as he pointed down river. "This is definitely the place."

Lucas removed another two feet of sand until he hit bedrock. The wolf was gone!

"Who knew about this?" asked Mrs. Moore.

"Only our parents," replied Hailey. "We had to tell them, so they understood why the private investigator was asking us questions. But, Mrs. Moore, I'm positive our parents would not have told anyone."

"Who would benefit from moving the wolf?" asked Mrs. Moore.

"She was working with Rebulus, so maybe he found her and moved her some place," suggested Hailey.

"What would be the benefit?" asked Mrs. Moore.

Lucas decided it was time to use the power of intelligence and see if he could catch bits of intelligence floating above his head. He turned the pointer on the Power Ring and pressed the crystal. Almost immediately ideas started pouring into his mind and he shared them with Hailey and Mrs. Moore.

"Maybe Rebulus is going to kill some young woman who looks like Senka and then plant some evidence that connects me to her. Maybe he'll find someone to claim she's Senka and accuse me of trying to kill her. Prescott told me there are some people who want to stop me from using the Power Ring. Maybe that someone is Mallory's uncle from Europe. Maybe he's the one that's trying to get the power."

"Lucas, those are all terrible things," exclaimed Hailey.

"Are any of those ideas stronger than the rest?" asked Mrs. Moore.

"Yeah," said Lucas. "We need to find out who the man is in the security video. Out of all the bits and pieces of intelligence bumping into my head, I'm getting a strong impression that the man in the video talking with Senka is the key."

"Then I suggest you follow that impression," agreed Mrs. Moore.

"To help solve this mystery, I think Hailey should talk with the investigator," suggested Lucas.

"Yes, I think that will help," responded Hailey. "I can do that."

"Well, if you need my help in any way, just let me know," offered Mrs. Moore. "Let's put this pile of rocks back the way it was and return to school."

☼ ☼ ☼

When Hailey suggested that she talk with the investigator, Mallory was surprised. Hailey's offer was totally unexpected, but Mallory readily agreed.

Hailey even offered to come to Mallory's house and recommended that the investigator bring the video of the stranger who was talking with Senka at the bus station.

With a little help from Prescott, Hailey and Lucas learned how to take the next step beyond hearing each other's thoughts with mental telepathy. Prescott called it "visual telepathy." With both of their Power Rings set to mental telepathy, Lucas could close his eyes and be able to see what Hailey saw like he did with the hawk in Yosemite. They decided it would be useful that while Hailey was talking with the investigator at Mallory's house, Lucas would be just across the street in his own home listening and watching everything.

When Hailey and her mom arrived at Mallory's house, the investigator was waiting in the living room. Caleb Fairbanks had been working investigations as a detective since he was twenty-four and then as a private investigator for the last ten years. He had seen it all and was sure a little ten-year-old girl would be easy to manipulate to get the answers he needed.

"Hello Hailey," said Caleb. "Thanks for helping with the investigation. Maybe you know something that will lead us to Mallory's aunt. Can you tell me what you remember about the camping trip in the desert?"

"I remember seeing Mallory's aunt in a ghost town near where we camped," said Hailey. "But I didn't see her at the campsite."

"What were you doing in the ghost town?" asked Caleb.

"Well, our families went to the ghost town to explore, and while Lucas and I were walking around, I saw her slip into a cave," said Hailey confidently.

"Where was the cave?"

"It was under the ghost town," replied Hailey. "It was probably part of the old mine."

"That's interesting," said Caleb. "Lucas didn't say anything about seeing Senka in the ghost town."

Lucas had been listening to the conversation and now Hailey heard Lucas in her mind. *"Ask him if he actually questioned me about seeing Mallory's aunt,"* said Lucas.

"Mr. Fairbanks, did you ask Lucas about seeing Mallory's aunt at the camp site or at the ghost town?"

Caleb flipped back through the pages of notes he took when he interviewed Lucas. He started twitching his mouth back and forth as if that would help him find the answer. It became clear he couldn't find anything in his notes to catch Lucas or Hailey in a lie.

"It might be helpful if I could see pictures from the security camera at the bus station," suggested Hailey.

"Sure," said Caleb. "Let's look at the video on my computer."

He pulled the laptop from his briefcase, set it on the coffee table and clicked on the file with the video. Hailey and Mallory sat together on the couch and Caleb turned the computer screen toward the girls so they could see the video. Their moms looked over the shoulders of their daughters so they could also watch.

"What did the police say about the security video?" asked Hailey.

The question caught Caleb off guard. He was told by his employer to keep the police out of the investigation.

"The police haven't commented yet, but they gave me this copy to help with the investigation."

Hailey and Mallory watched the video that showed Senka getting off the bus and looking around.

"Are you seeing this Lucas?" asked Hailey.

"Yes," replied Lucas.

Senka disappeared from one video camera and reappeared in another. She started pacing back and forth as if she was nervous about something. After a minute, Senka turned and faced the camera as a man walked into view. He was about a head taller than Senka and was wearing a black hat that looked like a bowling ball with a curved brim all around. He was well-dressed in a dark gray jacket and pants. His clothing and white hair stood out as most of the other travelers had black hair and were dressed casually at the Barstow bus station. He held out his arms for a hug, but Senka stood still, her arms crossed. As their conversation continued, it was clear Senka was extremely upset. She was shaking her head and at one point, she held up her hand to tell the man to stop talking.

"Lucas, do you have any idea why Senka was so angry?" asked Hailey.

"I don't, but she seems to have taken her anger out on us in the desert."

"Mr. Fairbanks, do the police know who this man is?" asked Hailey

"No. The video never showed his face," replied Caleb.

Hailey watched the silent conversation between Senka and the mystery man and wished she knew how to read lips. Lucas was across the street in his own house with his eyes closed and was seeing everything Hailey saw. At the bus station, some people walked by with luggage and Senka and the man moved out of their way and closer to the building. He must have known the locations of the security cameras and was careful to ensure he never faced any camera. It was clear Senka was angry about something by the way she was moving her hands and pointing at the man. Hailey was concentrating on Senka's mouth hoping to figure out a few words. Senka pointed her finger at the man and Hailey thought Senka might be saying, *"You promised. You promised."*

That's when she heard Lucas in her mind. *"Stop the video! Go back and look at the reflection in the window.*

"Could you please back up the video?" asked Hailey.

"Why? What did you see?" asked Caleb

"I'm not sure," replied Hailey.

Caleb reversed the video to when the man walked into the view of the camera.

"Can you play it at a slow speed?" asked Hailey.

"Sure, but what did you see?" asked Caleb.

"Just watch," replied Hailey. "I'll tell you when to stop."

Caleb ran the video forward at half-speed wondering what this ten-year old girl could see that he might have missed. Caleb was irritated that a young kid like Hailey might be better at finding clues than he was.

"Stop right there!" exclaimed Hailey.

"Why? What is it?" asked Caleb.

"Look at the reflection in the window. That's the man you need to find," said Hailey.

"*Lucas, do you recognize the man in the reflection?*"

"*I sure do. We met him at Stonehenge in England. That's the man with the huge moustache. It's Alastair Janus! But what is he doing at the bus station with Senka?*"

Hailey saw Caleb Fairbanks looked confused as he stared at the man on the computer screen.

At last, he said, "That's Senka's father. He's the one who hired me to find her."

"Alastair's the one who hired you?" asked Mrs. Fontaine.

Without answering, Caleb picked up the computer so the girls couldn't see the screen. He wanted a closer look at the reflection in the window. He saw his employer, but he could not see a reflection of Senka. Instead, there was a large wolf snarling at the man wearing the gray suit. Mallory must have missed it, but Hailey and Lucas saw the wolf.

Caleb quickly closed the computer and shoved it into his briefcase. The color had drained from his face, and he was clearly troubled by what he saw.

"I'm sorry Mrs. Fontaine. I can no longer search for Senka. I will inform her father I am off the case."

Giving no reason, he left without another word. Mallory and her mom were confused, but Hailey figured the reflection of the wolf in the window was the reason Caleb Fairbanks left so quickly.

Caleb Fairbanks got into his truck and thought about what he had just seen in the video. He decided to take another look to make sure. He opened his computer and fast-forwarded to the scene with the reflection in the window. There it was. The reflection in the window, though dim, was the fiercest looking wolf he had ever seen. In all his years on the police force and as a private investigator, he had never come across anything this strange. He closed his computer and got out his phone to call the man who had hired him. Just then, his phone rang. He did not recognize the number but answered like he always did hoping for a new client.

"Caleb Fairbanks, P.I. What mystery can I solve for you today?"

"Hello Mr. Fairbanks," said a voice with an unmistakable British accent. Caleb had not figured out how he was going to drop Alastair Janus and was scrambling to know what to say.

"Mr. Fairbanks, I will no longer need your services," declared Alastair. "I have found my daughter, and all is as it should be."

Caleb tried to think about what that could actually mean. '*All is as it should be?*' Your daughter is a wolf and all's well! Caleb thought about his own daughter who was married with two kids and how that was normal. Who has a wolf for a daughter?

"Mr. Fairbanks, are you still there? Did you hear me?"

"Oh, yes, Mr. Janus. I heard you. Sorry, I was just distracted by the traffic." *The traffic in my head.* "I'm glad you found her."

"What is the final amount I owe you for your troubles?" inquired Alastair.

"You owe me nothing," replied Caleb. "Let's just consider the account paid in full and the investigation closed."

"Very well, Mr. Fairbanks. Thank you and goodbye."

Before Alastair hung up the phone, Caleb heard him say, "That's strange. He didn't even ask where I found you."

Thirteen

Results of Initiative

*The difference between impossible
and possible is determination.*

Lucas and Hailey arrived at school early again and found the teachers waiting.

"Where are we traveling today?" asked Hailey.

"Today we are going to Spain to visit with another member of the Light Bearer Council. She is a business professor in Madrid" replied Mrs. Moore. "Are you ready?"

They replied with a nod and held onto one another's arms in the square grip to begin the journey. When the bright lights and the rushing water faded away, they were standing in the shade of a grove of trees. The air was cool and dry. Lucas guessed it was late afternoon by the angle of the shadows. He saw people walking around with books and backpacks and realized they were at some school. On a bench nearby sat a beautiful woman with black hair and bronze skin. She stood to greet the travelers.

"Lucas and Hailey, let me introduce you to Sarianna Galindez." said Miss Miller.

"Buenas tardes mis jóvenes portadores de luz. Bienvenido a España."

"Good afternoon my young light bearers," repeated Sarianna.

"Good afternoon," said Lucas.

"Hola Senorita Galindez," said Hailey with a smile. "Donde estamos?"

"We are at the Saint Louis University in Madrid where I teach just southwest of my home in Charmatin."

"Mrs. Moore said you are professor of international business," said Hailey. "You seem too young and pretty to be a college professor."

"Gracias," replied Sarianna smiling. "You are too kind."

"How did you get to be a college professor and a Light Bearer?" asked Hailey

"Let me tell you a story."

Sarianna sat down on the bench and invited Lucas and Hailey to sit on the grass in front of her.

"I came to the United States from Spain when I was a young girl. My father took a teaching position at a university in California. When I was about twelve, I asked my parents about making some extra money. They suggested I talk with the neighbors to see if any wanted me to mow their lawns. I spoke with one elderly neighbor at the end of our street about my superb lawn mowing skills to convince her I would do an excellent job. She said she did need someone to mow her lawn but was not sure if she should hire a girl. I assured her I could work as hard as any boy and asked her to let me prove it. She agreed and said she would pay me according to the work I did. She said I could mow her lawn for five dollars or fifty dollars, depending on how much I did and the quality of my work."

"Wow! You got fifty dollars for mowing a lawn?" exclaimed Lucas.

"I know it sounds like a lot of money for just mowing a lawn," said Sarianna. "But I found out it was more than just mowing a lawn. It wasn't about the money, but something else I got that was much more valuable."

Lucas tried to imagine how she could be paid with something other than money.

"I started mowing her lawn that very day. When I finished, the woman came out to inspect the work and said it looked nice and it was worth about five dollars. She saw my disappointment and said to come back in two weeks to mow the lawn again.

"Two weeks later I arrived on the appointed day and was reminded I would be paid according to my initiative. I worked harder than I had ever worked. I mowed the lawn in one direction and then mowed in another direction to create a diamond pattern in the grass. I was on my hands and knees trimming the grass when Mrs. Bryant came out and gave me a glass of cold lemonade. She said I was doing a better job than last time.

"When I was finished, I knocked on her door. She came out and walked around her yard inspecting my work. She said it looks very nice and handed me a ten-dollar bill. I thanked her and asked what I needed to do for a fifty-dollar lawn job. She replied, 'That's for you to decide. And don't ask me if your work is good enough. If you must ask, then it isn't. Then with a smile and a twinkle in her eyes, she asked, 'See you in two weeks?'

"As I rode home, I saw a professional gardener and stopped to look at his work and got some ideas for the next time I went to Mrs. Bryant's home.

"Two weeks later, I hooked a wagon to my bike and loaded the wagon with supplies. I arrived early in the morning and started on my plan to earn fifty dollars. I looked through my mom's gardening book one more time for instructions before trimming the rose bushes just like in the pictures. I got poked a few times with the thorns, but I didn't mind as I had my goal fixed in mind.

"Next, I used the clippers to trim the hedge. I eyeballed the trim line to make sure there was not a single leaf out of place. I continued trimming and fertilizing the plants for the next three hours. After mowing the lawn in both directions and then at an angle, I went back over the entire lawn and trimmed any blade of grass standing too tall. I circled the entire lawn on my hands and knees to trim the edge of the grass with my hand clippers.

"It was midafternoon when I realized how hungry I was. I quickly ate my sandwich and apple and continued with raking and sweeping until there was not a single blade of grass or leaf on the ground. Mrs. Bryant had brought me water and lemonade several times during the day but said nothing about my work. Still, I thought I had seen the hint of a smile as she turned to go back into the house.

"Finally, I surveyed my work and was very pleased with my effort. The sun was setting behind the hills when I packed everything into my wagon. I was walking up to the front porch when Mrs. Bryant stepped out of the house. She walked around the yard inspecting everything I had done. She said she had employed a lot of gardeners in her life but there was never anyone who worked as hard or with greater commitment.

"Then, she looked me in the eye and stated, 'I have been saving this fifty-dollar bill for years and you are the first person to have earned it.'"

"She handed me the bill, winked and said, 'Please come to my home next Saturday morning, I have another job for you.'"

"I felt like I was floating on air, and I could do anything."

"What was the other job," asked Hailey excitedly.

"The following week, I learned that Mrs. Bryant was a Light Bearer and had chosen to teach me. That fifty-dollar lawn job was just the beginning of my training which has led me to serve on the Light Bearer council."

"Sarianna is very modest about her accomplishments," said Miss Miller. "After she was trained in the ways of the Light Bearers, she earned a business degree from Stanford University and moved back to Madrid to teach. She has also started several businesses to help students at the university."

"It's true," admitted Sarianna. "I have accomplished some wonderful things in my life. But if there is one idea I want you to take home, it's the importance of initiative. Sometimes the difference between impossible and possible is your initiative and determination to reach a goal. Mrs. Bryant taught me that years ago and it has made all the difference in my life."

"Thank you, Sarianna," said Mrs. Moore. "We need to get these two back to school."

"Before you leave, I would like you to meet a student who attends the university. This is my young Light Bearer in training, Antonio Rosario."

Lucas and Hailey stood up and turned around to greet a young man about sixteen years old.

"Hola mis amigos," said Antonio. "Sarianna has asked me to give you a key. She said you would know how to use this."

Lucas expected to be handed another key like the lightning bolts but instead Antonio just said, "The key is just three words."

Before Antonio could say anything, Lucas felt ominous darkness surround them. He could not see anything, he only felt it as Antonio was grabbing at unseen hands holding his throat and choking him. Lucas immediately tried to reach for his Power Ring to do something, anything, but his muscles would not obey his thoughts. Hailey looked at Lucas, also clearly paralyzed, her eyes were pleading for him to do something. She had never seen such a terrible expression of pain on his face.

Out of the corner of his eye, Lucas saw the teachers and expected help from them, but they too appeared to be paralyzed and motionless as well. Lucas heard Hailey in his mind. *"Remember the cave! Remember what you did in the cave!"*

Lucas closed his eyes and calmed his mind to the point where he could use telekinesis to turn the pointer for time jumping and focused on Antonio greeting them and squeezed hard on the crystal with his mind. Suddenly, they all jumped back in time exactly as Lucas had pictured it in his mind. He then quickly turned the pointer again and stopped time except for the six of them in the park. The students walking nearby, including two on bicycles were motionless like colorful statues.

"Thank you, Lucas!" exclaimed Miss Miller. "I have never felt the darkness that strong before. What did our empath feel?" as she looked at Mrs. Moore.

Mrs. Moore was quiet for a moment as the group waited for her response.

"I felt fear and anger and some sadness as well," said Mrs. Moore, "but mostly fear." "Whoever or whatever that was, does not want Lucas to hear those three words."

"That was not Rebulus," said Lucas. "I would have remembered his smell and that was not him. Do you think Rebulus has someone working with him?"

"I wouldn't be surprised," replied Sarianna. "We have some very mean and evil inhabitants in our city, but I have never encountered this one. Let's finish what you came to learn."

Lucas and Hailey turned to Antonio again. He was still shaking after being attacked and took a moment for a deep breath. Once he was calm, he said, "The key is this, 'inteligencia, luz, verdad,' spoken in that order. Maybe it's a password or something."

Hailey repeated the words, "Inteligencia, luz, verdad, is that right?"

"That's correct. And you totally nailed the accent. That was good," replied Antonio.

"What do the words mean?" asked Lucas.

"The words translate to intelligence, light, truth," said Antonio. "I wish you luck with whatever you need to do with this key. It was a pleasure to meet you, but I sure hope we don't have that experience again."

Lucas and Hailey turned to Sarianna, and she held out her open arms inviting a hug. She hugged Hailey then turned to Lucas and hugged him. There it was again. When he shook hands or hugged the Master Light Bearers, Lucas felt a jolt of electricity or a tingle as though he was being charged with power. That is, except for one. It felt like *that one* was taking power away.

Sarianna stepped back and put her hands on their shoulders and offered some final words. "Please commit those key words to memory but never ever say them out loud until you are asked to use these words as a key," cautioned Sarianna. "There are listening ears all around and this must remain our secret. Deja que tu luz siempre brille brillante. Let your light always shine bright."

Sarianna walked over to Antonio and put her arm around his shoulder and waved goodbye as they disappeared.

"Being surrounded by that darkness was not the lesson we had planned for today," said Miss Miller. Lucas, I suggest you talk with Prescott about what happened today when you get home. Speaking of home, it's time to go.

☼ ☼ ☼

That afternoon, when Lucas got home, he grabbed a couple of crickets and released them into Prescott's cage even though Prescott was sitting on top of his cage. Lucas stood staring at Prescott for a moment and then smiled.

"What is causing you to smile my friend? Did you have a good day?" asked Prescott.

"I'm smiling because I realized you really don't need a cage. You are not going to escape unless you want to. And if you did want to, no cage is going to stop you."

"You are correct. I do not need a cage. But I do like the leaves and the climbing branches. It is the crickets that need the cage, so I do not have to chase them very far. Lucas, behind your smile, I see some concern on your face," said Prescott. "What happened today?"

Lucas told Prescott what happened in Spain and their experience with the darkness that was so strong and overpowering even the teachers couldn't help. I finally calmed my mind enough to use the Power Ring to time jump.

"I think there are more evil forces that want the Power Ring," concluded Lucas.

"It goes much deeper than someone trying to steal your Power Ring or taking your light. There are forces that are trying to prevent you from bringing additional light to the world. Word is spreading that there is a Light Bearer with the birthright who is becoming stronger each day. They fear they will lose the power and control they have,"

"That's what Mrs. Moore said today. She said she could feel the darkness was angry but mostly it was fearful," said Lucas.

"There are some people, maybe even some Light Bearers, who have been confused by the darkness. The only power that can save them is light. Light and dark cannot occupy the same space at the same time," said Prescott.

"You mean like when I go into a dark room and turn on the light, the darkness is gone?"

"That is exactly right. Always let your light shine bright. Lucas, be watchful of those who want to steal your light and leave you in the dark."

Fourteen

Leaving Normal Behind

If you only want to be normal, you will never know how really amazing you can be.

"*Lucas, we need to talk.*"

"What do you want, Prescott?" said Lucas sleepily. It was not unusual for Prescott to wake Lucas in the middle of the night to have important discussions. Lucas opened one eye and was amazed to see the glow-in-the-dark stars on his ceiling were still very bright. He searched for the numbers on the clock. It was almost three in the morning.

"What is it, Prescott? It's the middle of the night."

"*I'm not Prescott. It's Grandpa Lightfoot.*"

That was enough of a shock to get Lucas to open both eyes, sit up and listen. Grandpa Lightfoot had died before Lucas was born. Lucas looked around the room but saw no one.

"Grandpa Lightfoot, is it really you? Where are you?" asked Lucas. "How is this possible?"

It was almost a year ago when Lucas was given the Lightfoot Family History book by the substitute school librarian. That day Lucas learned he could actually talk with his ancestors. Now his Grandpa John Lightfoot, who had died before he was born, was calling to him.

"Lucas, come get my picture that's hanging on the wall in the hallway and bring it back to your room. We have important things to discuss."

Lucas was now fully awake. He crept to the hall where he found Grandpa Lightfoot's picture. Lucas carefully lifted the picture from the hooks and tiptoed back to his room. The sound of his dad's snoring pierced his parent's bedroom door and came drifting down the hallway like a noisy intruder. Lucas hoped his mom and dad would stay asleep because he did not want to try to explain why he had his grandpa's picture in his room.

Lucas quietly closed his bedroom door, set the picture on his desk, and leaned it against the wall. Lucas turned on his desk lamp and the colors in the photograph of Grandpa Lightfoot became more vivid than Lucas had remembered. The photograph quickly changed as Grandpa Lightfoot began talking as though he was alive and on a video call. Lucas thought his Grandpa Lightfoot looked a lot like his own dad, but with dark gray hair and glasses.

"Hello Lucas. I have been looking forward to meeting you for a long time."

Grandpa's tone of voice was soft and very loving. Lucas could feel the tenderness in Grandpa's words. Any other boy would not find this conversation normal at all, but Lucas had left normal behind long ago when he met Prescott. Even though Lucas was getting accustomed to the magical things in his life, he was still amazed when they happened - and this was no exception. Lucas had never met his Grandpa Lightfoot and wondered why he was visiting him now.

"This is so amazing!" whispered Lucas. "I can actually talk to my grandpa! I wish I could have met you before you died. Dad has told me many times you were a wonderful father and how much he loved you."

"*I feel the same way about you,*" said Grandpa Lightfoot. "*Although we did not meet when you were born, I have been watching over you with great interest.*"

"What do you mean? Why have you been watching over me?"

"The Light Bearer Council has known for many years there would be someone, who, because of the birthright, would have the power to recover the Sun Stone. Lucas, because both Grandpa Jack and I are Light Bearers, you have the birthright. You are the one with the right to recover the Sun Stone and unlock the power it holds."

"What's a Sun Stone, Grandpa?"

"Although the Sun Stone is small, it is the most powerful crystal created for a Power Ring. You had a conversation with Captain John Lightfoot in your family history book. Do remember?"

"Sure," replied Lucas in a whisper. "He was my thirteenth great-grandfather."

"That's correct. Captain Lightfoot was the first in our family to be trained as a Light Bearer and was the first recipient of the Sun Stone."

"Where did he get it?"

"The Sun Stone was given to him by the elders in the Powhatan tribe in Virginia. Many of the early settlers did not understand the Indians, but Captain Lightfoot did, and he treated them with respect. As a result of his honest dealings with the Powhatan Indians, they gave him the Sun Stone and the power to use it. From the Powhatans, John learned the true source of the power of the Sun Stone was simply obeying the laws of nature. These Native Americans knew so much more about

nature and the natural science behind what most see as magic."

"Wow! I didn't realize there were so many Light Bearers in the family."

"The Sun Stone was passed down through the generations, but when my father was about your age, it was hidden."

"Hidden? Why was it hidden? Wasn't it supposed to go to you?" asked Lucas.

"Yes, it was, but it was hidden for a good reason."

"What happened?" whispered Lucas.

"Over the years, the number of Light Bearers increased, and the Council was formed with the purpose of selecting and training new Light Bearers. Most of the council members were good, but one of the leaders on the council wanted to control the power of the Sun Stone and stole the Power Ring. Unfortunately, she was being influenced by the demon Vilonious."

"Who was Vilonious?" asked Lucas.

"He was a cunning demon who led many good people into the darkness, including some very skilled Master Light Bearers. I believe you have had some dealings with the son of Vilonious."

"I have? Who was it?"

"You know him as Rebulus."

"Oh, wow! Yes, we have met a few times, but, truthfully, Grandpa, I'd rather not see him again."

Grandpa Lightfoot chuckled. *"Yes, Lucas, I don't blame you. Vilonious was obsessed with power and wanted to control the Sun Stone to use it for evil purposes. We heard that he either killed the Light Bearer who had stolen the Sun Stone, or she drowned herself."*

"How did they get it back?"

"A young Light Bearer by the name of Liam Kincaid volunteered to capture and return the Sun Stone."

"I met him in England," said Lucas excitedly, "but I can't imagine him ever being young."

"Oh, he was young once, Lucas, I can assure you! Kincaid fought Vilonious the Light Thief and finally killed him. After their experience with Vilonious, the Light Bearer Council decided to protect the Sun Stone. They did this by locking it away in Wat Arun, the Temple of Dawn in Thailand, knowing that one day there would be a Light Bearer with the birthright who was able to use the Sun Stone. Lucas, you are that Light Bearer.

"Wow!" gulped Lucas, feeling the weight of his grandfather's words.

"The keys to retrieving the Sun Stone were then sent all over the world so there would never be one person with all of the keys until now. The legend is told among the Light Bearers that the monkey ate the Sun Stone."

"What does that mean, the monkey ate the Sun Stone?"

"I actually don't know, Lucas. But I suppose it's a clue to finding the Sun Stone," replied Grandpa Lightfoot.

"How am I supposed to get it?" asked Lucas. "I've never been to Thailand or the Temple of Dawn."

"Well, until last week, you had never been to Africa, England or Spain," reminded Grandpa.

"Will I be going with Miss Miller and Mrs. Moore again?"

"No, this time Prescott will take you and Hailey. The Light Bearers, who hid the Sun Stone, have given Prescott instructions on where to find it. You have already been given the keys to unlock the vault where the Sun Stone is hidden."

"I have?"

"Yes. You received the first key in Africa from Michael Naidoo. The coins you and Hailey received become a key when used together. The second key was given to you in England by Liam Kincaid and Megan Demeter. Do you and Hailey still have those keys?"

"Yes, of course we have them," replied Lucas.

"Marvelous! You received the third key in Spain from Antonio Rosario. Do you remember the words?" asked Grandpa Lightfoot.

"Yes, the words are... oops! I almost forgot. I can't say the words out loud until I get to wherever the Sun Stone is hidden. So, how will we get to Thailand without Mrs. Moore and her blue crystal?"

"Prescott has a similar but more powerful crystal on his collar, and he will be your guide," replied Grandpa Lightfoot. *"Once there, you will meet a young man and he will help you recover the Sun Stone."*

"How will we find him?"

"Don't worry about finding him. He'll find you."

As he thought about all that Grandpa Lightfoot had told him about Light Bearers and Vilonious dying, Lucas felt the tremendous weight of what he was being asked to do. He was beginning to have that feeling again, the one where he was not excited about being the hero and having the responsibility of the birthright. He was feeling overwhelmed by what seemed to be a task only he could complete. He wasn't even sure what it meant to have the birthright. And he didn't know where Thailand was. It could be on the moon for all he knew. Lucas sat on his bed as he thought about the burden of being a Light Bearer. Tears began to well up in his eyes.

"I'm just a kid! What if I mess up? What if I can't get the Sun Stone?"

"Lucas," said Grandpa tenderly, *"I understand what you're feeling. I started my journey as a Light Bearer when I was your age, and I was scared too. It all seemed too much for me as well. But I got through it. Lucas, you were born with a special light inside of you, and that spark of goodness will give light to many others. But it's still your choice."*

"But what if I just want to be ordinary and normal?"

"If all you ever want to be is normal, you will never know how really amazing you can be."

Lucas had been given a lot of cool powers with the Power Ring but there was one power Prescott had not given him. It was a power he had to give himself. That was the power of choice. Lucas realized he could choose to be a Light Bearer or just a normal boy. He could choose to help others or not. He could choose to bring light to others or sit in darkness. He felt like a reluctant hero, but he still had a choice. Lucas stood up and turned off the lamp on his desk. The only light in the room came from the nightlight and the bright stars glowing on the ceiling. The stars absorbed the light and now glowed in the dark.

"What are you thinking?" asked Grandpa.

"See those stars on the ceiling? The ones that shine the brightest in the dark are the ones directly above the light because that's where the light was brightest. I just realized I am like the desk lamp. I can let my light shine bright for the benefit of others or I can be part of the darkness. I don't know how this will happen, but there seems to be a lot of people who have more faith in me than I have in myself. If you and Grandpa Jack and Katrina and Prescott all believe in me, then I guess I should believe and have faith in myself."

"Lucas, let me give you something to think about," said Grandpa. *"Faith is not a leap into the dark, but a step into the light. Each step you take in*

the right direction, will light up the darkness. A time will come when you understand what this means."

Lucas sat quietly for a moment looking back at the stars on his ceiling. He knew what he must choose and asked, "When do we leave for Thailand?"

"You and Hailey can leave tomorrow after school," said Grandpa Lightfoot. *"By the way, Thailand is on the other side of the world just above the equator."*

Lucas crept back to the hall with the picture of Grandpa Lightfoot and quietly replaced the picture on the wall when he heard his grandpa whisper to him.

"Lucas, please remember, you are not alone. You have family and friends around to help you whenever you need help. You don't need to carry this responsibility alone. Get some sleep. You have a big day ahead of you."

Fifteen

Reality is Simply an Illusion

Turn problems into possibilities and obstacles into opportunities

Lucas was a little nervous about going on a trip without the teachers, so he was glad Prescott was going with them to Thailand. Lucas and Hailey had instructions to meet with Katrina in the classroom after school. To prepare for the trip, they were to bring the keys they had received along with their Power Rings. Hailey was looking at a world map on the wall when Katrina came into the classroom.

"Hi Katrina," said Hailey excitedly. "Did you know Thailand is almost eight thousand miles from California across the Pacific Ocean?"

"I did, Hailey! In fact, I have been there, and I know the young man you will meet in Thailand. His name is Andrew Bastion, and he is one of the happiest people I know. He will almost certainly have a smile on his face."

"Where are we meeting him?" asked Hailey.

"Andy will meet you in Bangkok at the Wat Arun Temple and he will help Prescott find the monkey and the Sun Stone," replied Katrina.

"What do you mean, 'find the monkey'?" questioned Hailey.

Without answering the question, Katrina continued, "Andy and Prescott will show you the location in the temple where the Sun Stone is hidden. Do you have your keys?"

"Yes," replied Hailey.

"Me too," replied Lucas.

"And do you have your Power Rings?" asked Katrina.

"Yes," they both replied in unison.

"Good, you're all set then. I'm sure you will do great," assured Katrina. "Stay with Prescott and Andy and they will protect you."

"Speaking of Prescott where is he?" asked Hailey.

"I am right here," replied Prescott.

They turned to see Prescott on the desk next to Miss Harrison with Lucas's green shoulder pack.

"How did you get here?" asked Lucas.

"You might recall, the cage is for my crickets and not my containment," reminded Prescott. *"Are you two ready to go?"*

Lucas knew there was no risk in virtual reality, but he had an odd feeling the trip to Thailand would be dangerous. He took a deep breath and let it out with a sigh, "Ready when you are."

Hailey nodded in agreement.

Miss Harrison handed Lucas his green shoulder pack and he put it over his head with the strap across his chest. Prescott jumped from the desk and landed on Lucas's shoulder and gripped the strap with his claw-like feet.

"Please take care of our young Light Bearers," said Miss Harrison.

"Keeping them safe is more important than securing the Sun Stone, but I will do both," promised Prescott.

Lucas and Hailey used both of their hands and arms to form the square grip as instructed and held onto one another's wrists just above the passport bracelets. Lucas forced the feeling of fear from his mind by standing a little taller, holding his head a little higher and smiling. It was just the two of them with their hands and arms locked in place for the journey. Standing eye to eye they couldn't help but grin at each other knowing how exciting these virtual trips could be.

"Are you ready for another adventure?" asked Hailey.

Lucas nodded. He wondered how long this trip might take and made a mental note that it was three o'clock in the afternoon when the crystal on Prescott's collar began to glow blue.

"Hang on tight," said Prescott as he winked at Hailey.

The light spread out until Lucas and Hailey were encircled in a huge cobalt-colored glowing ball. Points of light, like dancing fireflies, began circling around the outside of their protective bubble. They were spinning in all directions like millions of tiny stars.

"*This trip is definitely going to be different,*" thought Lucas.

Hailey nodded in agreement with a wide-eyed look of excitement. Lucas wondered if Hailey might be frightened; he noticed her grip on his arm had tightened quite a bit. They heard the familiar sound of rushing water, but this time there was a strong wind that blew Hailey's long hair all around and she wished she had worn her hair in a ponytail. After what might have been a few seconds, the wind slowed, and Hailey's long hair floated around in slow motion like she was under water.

Lucas had no idea of how long they were traveling on light, but rather than count the seconds, he just enjoyed the journey. When the bright light faded and the wind and sound ceased, they found themselves standing in front of an enormous building. It was shaped something like a pyramid with a tall spire in the center. In the four corners, there were shorter spires. It reminded Lucas of the Matterhorn at Disneyland but twice as tall. The building was outlined against the gray morning sky. Even without much light, Lucas could see that the Wat Arun Temple was very elaborate with strange carvings. The sun had not yet risen, and Lucas thought it might be about five o'clock in the morning.

"Is this the Wat Arun Temple?" asked Hailey.

"Good morning, my friends. Yes, it is and, by the way, its name means the Temple of Dawn."

The cheerful voice came from their right and the travelers turned to see the young man Katrina had said would meet them. Andy was waiting on the steps and when he stood, he was about a foot taller than Lucas, He had a full face and short dark hair. He wore a short-sleeve white shirt with double pockets and tan shorts. His shoes looked like a cross between tennis shoes and sandals.

"Welcome to Thailand, the land of smiles. Prescott, it's so good to see you my old friend. You must be Lucas and Hailey. I'm so excited to finally meet you. My name is Andrew Bastion, but my friends call me Andy."

Andy came forward and gave Lucas and Hailey each a hug as if they had been long lost friends he hadn't seen in years. Lucas felt an instant connection to Andy. He could sense there was something very special about him, even more so than with the Light Bearers in other countries. Andy noticed a perplexed look on Lucas's face.

"Is something wrong Lucas?"

"No. Um, well I thought we'd be meeting someone who was from Thailand sort of like the Light Bearers we've met in the other countries. But you don't have an accent," replied Lucas.

"Thailand is my adopted home," said Andy. "I was actually born in California but came to Thailand to teach English. In the process I made many wonderful friends. I fell in love with the people, the culture, the food. And I even married a beautiful young Thai woman. I am very happy here and feel like this is where I belong. I have even started to eat like Prescott."

"What do you mean?" asked Hailey. "Do you eat crickets too?"

"Yes, and they are delicious!" said Andy with a laugh. "One of my favorite foods is deep fried crickets seasoned with chili pepper."

"Mmmm! That sounds absolutely delicious," said Prescott.

"Yuck! You've got to be kidding!" exclaimed Hailey.

Her response only made Andy laugh harder.

"Hailey, crickets are an excellent source of protein. You should try them some time," suggested Prescott.

"Oh! No thank you!" said Hailey. "I think I'll pass."

"I am afraid we must hurry everyone. We do not have much time. We must get to the vault as the sun rises," said Prescott.

"Andy, do you know the location of the monkey on the East side?"

"I do. It's near the top on the far side," replied Andy. "Lucas, you should go first, Hailey can follow you and I'll be last."

"Go where?" asked Lucas.

"We need to climb up these stairs," replied Prescott. *"We need to get to the stone monkey near the top before the sun comes up."*

Lucas looked up at the very steep, almost endless stairs.

"Wow! These steps are really steep! Are you sure we won't fall off?" asked Lucas.

"Prescott, can't you just teleport us up to the top or something?" asked Hailey. "It would be a lot easier."

"I could, but you would miss seeing all of the intricate carvings along the way to the top of the temple," replied Prescott.

"I notice you get to ride," muttered Hailey under her breath.

Lucas looked at Hailey with a weak smile hoping for some encouraging words, but she just set her face to determined, glanced upward and moved toward the steps.

"After you, Lucas," said Hailey. "You get to lead the way."

Lucas began climbing and stopped every twenty to thirty steps to look back to see how Hailey was doing. Because the steps were so steep, he was worried about Hailey falling. He looked to the West at the one and two-story buildings with their red, blue, and gray tiled roofs just beyond the temple grounds. He realized they were the only ones at the temple this early in the morning; the city of Bangkok was just waking up. Lucas suddenly had a feeling of apprehension as though something terrible was going to happen. Something wasn't quite right, but Lucas couldn't put his finger on it.

Prescott could sense Lucas becoming more anxious and said, *"Keep going Lucas. You are doing fine."*

"Lucas, when we get to the top of this last set of stairs, I want you to turn to the right," directed Andy. "Then we'll go around to the east side of the temple."

When Lucas arrived at the walkway at the top of the stairs, he turned and reached down to help Hailey up the last tall step. Andy was not far behind, and he bounded up the stairs with great enthusiasm. The uneven stone walkway was about two feet wide which required them to walk single file. There was no hand railing to hold on to for balance or safety which caused Lucas to be even more concerned. The right side of the walkway dropped off about twenty feet to the stone below.

"Please be very careful," warned Andy. "Stay away from the edge of the walkway. It drops off to the statues below and if you fell over the ledge, you would probably not survive the fall."

Lucas thought it was strange for Andy to warn them about danger since this was a virtual trip. With Prescott still on his shoulder, Lucas followed the walkway to the corner nearly hugging the wall and turned left toward the East. The river below the temple came into view.

"Prescott, there is something really unusual about this virtual trip," said Lucas. "I know we are still in the classroom but being here in Thailand seems so real. The air is really humid, and the odors are so different from anything I have ever smelled."

"Lucas, it feels real because this is not a virtual trip. We really are in Thailand."

"Wait, what? This is real?" exclaimed Lucas as he stopped with his back to the wall.

"In a virtual trip, you would not be able to retrieve the Sun Stone and return it to your home, so it was necessary to physically travel here."

"What's going on?" asked Hailey as she caught up to Lucas and Prescott. She was still out of breath after the strenuous climb.

"Prescott just told me this is not a virtual trip, and we are actually in Thailand," replied Lucas.

"You mean we're not at home in our classroom? Why?" asked Hailey nervously.

"*Hailey,*" replied Prescott calmly, "*With the help of the teachers, you and Lucas were given keys from the other Light Bearers you met on your virtual trips. To unlock the vault and retrieve the Sun Stone, you actually had to be here in Thailand.*"

"So how did we get here? Is it something like teleportation?"

"Hailey, there are some things scientists do not understand that Light Bearers have known for years. I do not have time to explain everything now, but in time you will know. What is important is that we are

running out of time and must get to the Sun Stone quickly," insisted Prescott.

They continued toward the East side of the temple, but with greater caution. As they walked, they were passing some very ugly statues that were carved in a pose as if they were holding up the building. The statues were about twelve feet tall and built to resemble strong warriors in battle armor. They had ugly monkey-like masks with big teeth and a big nose. Lucas would be glad to get away from these monkey-warriors looking down on them. Lucas reached the south-east corner of the temple and looked down to the river below. There were a few long narrow boats loaded with baskets of produce for the markets. Lucas looked toward the sunrise.

"What is that?" asked Lucas pointing toward the East. "It looks like a huge flock of black birds."

Everyone looked toward the direction that Lucas pointed and watched with curiosity. The black cloud approached and grew larger. At first it appeared to be black birds, but the closer they came, they all saw they were not birds at all.

"Those aren't birds. It's actually a colony of bats from the nearby caves," said Andy. "We call them flying foxes because their faces look just like a fox. In fact, they are one of the largest species of bats in the world."

"I thought bats only fly at night and sleep during the day," said Hailey.

"That is correct Hailey," said Prescott. There was concern in his words.

"These bats are here for only one reason, to block the sun. We need the sun to unlock the vault. It appears someone is controlling them. Our visit here today is not the secret I had hoped. Knowledge of our trip was limited to only a few of the Master Light Bearers and the Council. This confirms what I had suspected. There may be someone on the council who is trying to stop Lucas from getting the Sun Stone."

Andy focused his eyes on the bats and said, "This is not normal. They rarely fly during the day and never in such a large colony. Someone must be using powerful magic to control them. Let me take care of the bats," said Andy as he looked down to the river. "I have an idea."

Andy turned to face the river and closed his eyes. He put the palms of his hands together and stretched his arms toward the river. Lucas wondered what he was doing and why he was taking so long. The bats were getting closer, and he really didn't want to come face to face with a "flying fox". The colony of bats was so thick their shadow would soon cover the eastern side of the temple.

Hailey was watching where Andy was pointing and saw a large ball of water come up out of the river. She quietly tapped Lucas on the shoulder and pointed toward the river. He saw it too and nodded. They watched as the ball of water rose from the river and circled around the center spire of the temple and sped eastward toward the bats. A few bats in front of the colony were close enough for Lucas to see they had large red eyes and sharp teeth. Hailey saw them too.

Lucas turned to Hailey and said, "Do these bats look familiar?"

"Yeah," said Hailey. "They look more like a flying wolf than a fox. They also look like they're possessed, like someone has control over them."

As the ball of water flew passed the temple, there was a high-pitched whistling sound and Lucas noticed the water was separating into large droplets. The water droplets became longer and thinner and suddenly froze into tiny icicles that were aimed right at the bats. As the icy darts pierced each of bats, they just fell from the sky. Some bats fell into the river, below.

"That was so cool!" exclaimed Lucas.

Andy smiled and said, "That's how you take a problem and create a solution to benefit others."

"What do you mean?" asked Hailey. "It looks like you made a mess in the river. The flying foxes are now floating foxes."

"It won't be a mess for long. Listen and watch carefully."

Hailey and Lucas could hear Andy in their minds as he called out to the snakes and the otters in and around the river east of Wat Arun. Almost immediately, they saw splashing on the surface of the water as hundreds of otters began feasting on the bats. Within moments, they saw a stream of snakes slithering to the edge of the river and diving in for an early morning breakfast.

"That should do it," exclaimed Andy. The bats are gone, and the snakes and otters are getting a free meal. Everyone is happy."

As Lucas watched in amazement at Andy's skill at communicating with the animals and creating a solution to a mess, he heard Prescott in his mind.

"Lucas, that is a skill you too will develop on your journey to becoming a Master Light Bearer."

Sixteen

Quest for the Sun Stone

*Reality is created in the mind before
it is seen with the eye.*

The Light Bearers had climbed the steep steps on the west side of the temple and were making their way around the east side which overlooked the river.

"*Come. We have a mission to complete. There is a short window of time before the sun rises too high,*" urged Prescott.

"You will find the monkey centered between the two warrior guards." directed Andy.

They continued to the center of the east side of the temple and stopped between two of the ugly warrior guards, that's how Lucas thought of them, statues that were about six feet apart. He hoped they were there to scare away evil. The wall between the two statues was set back about four feet which provided more room for them to stand than the narrow ledge they were on before. Carved into the wall was a statue of a monkey chiseled in stone. The palms of the monkey were held out ready to hold something. Unlike the ugly warrior statues, this monkey was smiling.

"Place the coins you received from Michael into the eyes of the monkey with the lion and gazelle standing up and we will wait for the sun to rise," said Prescott.

In the center of each eye was a square crystal the exact size and shape to fit the hole in the center of the coins. Lucas put his coin on the monkey's right eye and Hailey put her coin on the left eye. With his hand shading his eyes, Lucas looked eastward to see how far the sun had risen.

"Guys, we may have another problem," announced Lucas.

There were storm clouds rising in the distance blocking the sun and once again the group was in shadow.

"Someone is definitely determined to stop us," said Prescott. *"Hailey, it is your turn to show us what you can do to remove the clouds."*

"Why me?" asked Hailey.

"You are the one with power over weather," replied Prescott.

"I am?" questioned Hailey.

"The symbol of a cloud on your Power Ring allows you to have power over the weather," reminded Prescott.

"Oh, I forgot about that symbol. What do I do?" asked Hailey.

"With the pointer toward the symbol of the cloud, focus your mind on what it would take to remove the

storm clouds and squeeze the crystal," instructed Prescott.

Hailey pulled the Power Ring from her pants pocket. She felt inadequate with the weight of this unexpected responsibility thrust onto her. She turned the pointer to the symbol of the cloud and pressed the crystal between her thumb and fingers. She wondered if she could really do what Prescott had asked. Then she heard the soothing voice of Prescott speaking slowly in her mind.

"Calm yourself, Hailey. Relax. Eliminate all distractions. You have been entrusted with this power for a reason. This is your gift. This is your contribution to the quest for the Sun Stone."

Hailey closed her eyes and allowed a feeling of confidence and assurance wash over her. The sounds of Bangkok disappeared and all she heard was the slow rhythmic beating of her heart. The dominant thought going through her mind was *'wind moves clouds, wind moves clouds.'*

With her eyes closed, she created a picture in her mind. It was a clear, bright, and sharply focused image with sounds and smells. She made it a colorful picture where she could feel and see the wind she desired. She imagined a warm breeze moving directly towards the storm clouds. As she focused on the outcome of what she wanted to accomplish – a clear blue sky - the breeze turned into a gusting wind and then into a much stronger airstream.

The tops of the trees were being whipped by the gusts of wind and a low whistling sound filtered down from the top of the temple. She then imagined a hurricane-force tempest without the rain. In her mind she imagined the clouds being blown away and dissolving into thin air.

"It's working Hailey!" exclaimed Lucas. "The clouds are moving!"

Hailey opened her eyes to see the last of the storm clouds dissolving and disappearing. She felt the warmth of the sun's rays on her face. The eastern horizon was cloud-free, and everyone was smiling at her.

"Wow! I did it! I destroyed the clouds!"

"That was amazing!" praised Lucas. "How does it feel to have that much power?"

"It feels kind of good, but at the same time, it's actually scary," replied Hailey.

"Let us continue," instructed Prescott. *"Put the second key into the groove in the palms of the monkey's hands."*

Lucas and Hailey removed the chain from around their necks and placed the second key, the lightning bolts, into the monkey's hands. Immediately, the light from the morning sun reflected through the crystals in the monkey's eyes and shot two laser beams of light to the two lightning bolts in the palms of the monkey's hands.

"Lucas, it is time for the final key. You may now say the words of the third key," said Prescott.

Suddenly, before Lucas could open his mouth, the two warrior guard statues on either side of him came to life! In a flash, one warrior picked up Lucas and held him by his arm dangling him out over the ledge. The other statue knocked Andy down with one arm and pushed him down onto the walkway and held him there with his foot. With the other arm, the warrior grabbed Hailey by her leg and now held her upside down over the edge.

Hailey was screaming and Lucas tried unsuccessfully to kick his legs up and wrap them around the stone arm so he wouldn't drop. Lucas could hear Andy groaning under the force of the warrior's stone foot that held him captive. If either Lucas or Hailey were dropped, they would likely die as they fell on the stone statues below. Suddenly, they all heard a deep gravelly voice, the unmistakable voice of Rebulus the Light Thief.

"Prescott, give us the Sun Stone or your young Light Bearers will die!"

Lucas was terrified as he realized this was not a virtual trip and he and Hailey could actually die. Prescott was still on his shoulder and Lucas knew the power his chameleon mentor possessed. In the time they had become friends, Lucas had never seen Prescott angry or frustrated. That changed today.

"I really dislike having to destroy ancient and historical property, Rebulus, but this is the choice you

have given me because I will not let my friends perish," avowed Prescott. *"It is time you crawl back into your darkest cave as you have no power over us!"*

Prescott stood, raised his front legs, and let out a low growl. The sound came from deep inside Prescott and was directed at the statues. The intensity of the sound quickly grew and sounded like the rumbling of distant thunder getting closer and closer until suddenly, there was the loud crack of thunder. Immediately, the statues exploded into fine dust, and they began falling. Hailey let out a scream as they fell but stopped abruptly as she realized they were all floating in mid-air back to the walkway. Both Lucas and Hailey softly landed on their feet facing the monkey statue. Andy stood up and looked around for any other demon statue that might be brought to life by an unseen force.

"Lucas, the final key, please," instructed Prescott.

Lucas ignored the fact that he was covered in statue dust and repeated the key words he had memorized. In his mind, Lucas was thinking, intelligence, light, truth as he spoke the words, "Inteligencia, luz, verdad."

What followed was a sound of stone scraping against stone. The solid stone of the monkey's stomach now became an open door. Lucas looked inside and saw a red box resting on top of a stone pedestal. The red box looked something like a book with gold writing on the cover. It was about six inches square and one inch thick.

"Please open the box to ensure that the Sun Stone is still there," requested Prescott.

Lucas reached in and removed the box. He opened it and pulled out the Sun Stone.

Hailey let out an audible gasp. "It's beautiful!"

The Sun Stone crystal was centered in a ring of smooth polished silver. About an inch in diameter the radiant crystal glowed in shimmering colors of yellow, orange and red. The Sun Stone was centered inside a Power Ring of polished silver that had no symbols or markings on it. As Lucas held the Sun Stone, he felt a strange bond to it, like it was something he had lost a long time ago and now had recovered. Pictures flooded his mind of people who were dressed in clothes he had only seen in history books. He wondered if these were all Light Bearers who had at one time possessed the Sun Stone.

"I am satisfied. Return the Sun Stone to the box and put it inside your shoulder pack, Take the coins and the lightning bolts and put them into your pack as well," instructed Prescott. *"It is time I get you both home. There still might be danger here."*

"Do we need to climb down all those steps?" asked Hailey.

"Not this time," replied Prescott. *"We can depart the temple from where we stand. Besides, the temple is now open to visitors and I do not want to be seen by them."*

"I'm so delighted I was able to meet you and be a part of this adventure," beamed Andy as he reached out and hugged Lucas. Andy stepped back and looked thoughtfully at the young Light Bearer. "Lucas, many years ago, I was told that one day I would be called on to help the one with the birthright to claim the Sun Stone. This is that day. You have been chosen for a reason and I am confident you will become the leader you were destined to be."

Andy turned to Hailey and gave her a hug and with a smile, declared, "Lucas will need your help, Hailey. He will need someone he can trust with his life and that person is you. You are both always welcome for a longer visit to my land of smiles. We have many smiles, but today I leave you with my victory smile," he grinned brightly. "Take care of yourselves…and each other."

"Andrew, thank you for your help today," said Prescott.

"It has been an honor to serve with my brother and sister of Light. If I'm ever needed again, you know where to find me. Prescott, I have one final request."

"What can I do for you?"

"Prescott, tell my mother I am doing fine and not to worry about me. I am engaged in the mission, as always, to bring light to the world."

"I promise to tell her when I return," assured Prescott.

As they said goodbye to Andy, a light seemed to gather directly around him, and he looked like he was filled with light. He put his hands together and nodded peacefully to Lucas and Hailey. Instantly, the light stretched into a pillar, and he rose skyward in the light until he disappeared.

"It is time we depart as well," said Prescott.

That was the cue for Lucas and Hailey to form the square grip with their arms. They smiled at one another signaling they were glad to be going home. The protective bubble of light surrounding Prescott, Lucas and Hailey grew larger until they were fully enveloped. The lights, and wind and the sound of rushing waters were once again their traveling companions. This was something Lucas was beginning to enjoy. Eventually, the light and sound faded away and the wind ceased, and they were back in the classroom. They were home! Lucas looked at the clock. It was ten minutes after three. They had only been gone for ten minutes, but it felt like hours. Lucas looked at his shirt and pants and saw the dust from the statues and knew they had been to Thailand with Andy. Lucas wondered how he was going to explain the dust all over his clothes and hair to his mother.

"Welcome home," said Miss Harrison. "I trust you were successful."

"*Yes, we were,*" replied Prescott. *"Hailey learned to use her new power over weather, and she has also learned that whatever she thinks in her mind becomes reality. Lucas learned there are forces which do not want him to have possession of the Sun Stone. And, despite the treacherous efforts of these dark forces, Lucas has succeeded in taking possession of the Sun Stone. Now the real challenge begins."*

"Now the real challenge begins?" rasped Hailey astonished.

All the wonderful thoughts of being home and getting back to a normal day faded when Lucas tried to imagine what Prescott meant.

"What do you mean the real challenge begins?" asked Lucas. "What could be more challenging after today?"

"Lucas and Hailey, I realize that the events of this day, this trip to Thailand, have been a very big challenge for you. This is a very important day in the history of Light Bearers. Both of you rose to the challenge to retrieve the Sun Stone, hidden for many years. But truly, it is only the beginning, as there are many more challenges ahead."

"Do not be discouraged, my friends," added Prescott, as he saw Lucas and Hailey exchange dismayed glances, "*Remember, we do not succeed in spite of our challenges, but precisely because of them."*

Seventeen

Time is Running Out

Only in the light can you judge the truth.

"We have got to the get the Power Rings! We are running out of time," exclaimed Damian. "Rebulus gave us thirty days and we only have a few days left."

"I know," replied Tanis, upset. "I didn't think it would take us this long. I really enjoy being human and I definitely don't want to go back to being a snake!"

"Me neither! But listen. I have an idea on how we can use Mallory to steal Hailey's Power Ring and then use her ring to get the Power Ring from Lucas."

When Hailey walked into class, Mallory was sitting in Hailey's desk talking quietly with Tanis and Damian. Damian said something to Mallory as Hailey approached and Mallory stood up and sat at her own desk.

"Hey Hailey, how's it going?" asked Mallory.

"Good. How are you?"

Mallory said she was fine just as the bell rang and all the kids who were standing, quickly moved to their seats. The only empty seats belonged to Lucas and a boy named Maverick Bright.

Maverick was one of the cool kids in the class. He was friendly with everyone and always said something funny when he stood in front of the class to give a report. He often talked about surfing with his dad. During one report, he said he was building a sandcastle at home from all the sand he collected from his ears after surfing.

He was a lot like Lucas. He was especially kind and respectful of others. He also seemed to have a light about him especially when he smiled. Although Miss Harrison never said anything about Maverick, Hailey sometimes wondered if he could also be a Light Bearer. His last name was Bright, so it seemed to fit.

Ever since Hailey "shape-shifted" and appeared as Mallory to the twins in the library, Hailey didn't trust Tanis or Damian and tried to avoid them outside of the classroom. That was hard to do sitting next to Damian, so in class, she tried to be friendly with the twins to avoid any suspicion.

Hailey noticed that over the last two weeks, Mallory was hanging around the twins a lot more during recess and lunch. She and Lucas had been busy with Miss Miller and Mrs. Moore after school with the training sessions and neither of the children had spent much time with Mallory.

Mallory leaned over the empty chair and whispered to Hailey, "Lucas isn't here today. Do you know where Lucas is?"

Hailey shook her head but knew she could find out with mental telepathy.

Lucas had a hard time getting up for school and persuaded his mom to let him stay home. It wasn't so much that he was sick, but he was feeling the weight of the responsibility of the Sun Stone. Besides, he didn't get much sleep thinking about what happened in Thailand. He was glad it ended okay and smiled every time he thought of Andy. Lucas was lying in bed when he heard Hailey in his mind.

"Lucas, are you at home?"

"Yes. I wasn't feeling well after yesterday's trip to Thailand."

"I think I know what you mean, especially thinking about how we almost died," replied Hailey.

"How are you handling it?" asked Lucas.

"I'm doing okay. You're the one with the birthright and all the responsibility that brings."

"Yeah, tell me about it! I'm still trying to understand it all. Will you please ask Mallory to bring me any homework assignments?"

"Sure," replied Hailey. *"I hope you feel better."*

When the lunch bell rang, Mallory invited Hailey to eat lunch with her. Although she was still cautious, Hailey agreed. They were sitting alone at one of the far tables when Tanis and Damian came and sat down next to them. Since Hailey rarely spoke with the twins outside of class, she assumed they were joining Mallory. Tanis sat next to Hailey and Damian sat across from his sister. As soon as they sat down Hailey had a bad feeling. She had the impression she should get up and walk away but thought it might be too rude and decided to stay. The conversation was pleasant at first, which may have been the reason Hailey let her guard down. They talked about the characters in the book Miss Harrison was reading with the class and how the author made the characters come to life.

Strangely, the twins started speaking to one another in a language Hailey did not recognize. The sound of their language was almost musical and wonderfully soothing. Hailey not only heard, but she felt a humming vibration that caused her to become very relaxed. She saw Mallory's eyes were open, but she seemed to be staring off into the distance. Mallory looked like a human robot as she picked at the grapes in her lunch. Hailey knew something was wrong as she struggled to have a clear thought.

She again had the impression to stand up and walk away, and started to get up, but her legs just wouldn't obey her thoughts.

"Focus girl! What are you doing here? Stand up and walk away!"

Although these were her thoughts, she just sat and listened to the musical conversation between the twins.

"What language are you speaking?" asked Hailey.

"It's called *Kundali*," replied Damian. "It's an old language our father taught us. As we speak, the words bypass the conscious mind and go directly into the unconscious mind."

Hailey was surprised that as Damian was speaking *Kundali* she could now clearly understand his words.

"I'm beginning to understand your language," exclaimed Hailey smiling.

"I see that you like our language," said Tanis.

"I do," replied Hailey. "It's wonderful!"

Hailey began to have a conversation with herself in her head. It was like two different halves of her brain talking to each other.

"Why did I say that?"

"You said that because it's a beautiful language. You like to learn new things. Maybe they can teach you their language."

"Beautiful or not, I need to get up. Go back to class. Go talk with Miss Harrison."

"Okay, you can in a minute. You need to finish your lunch."

Hailey's inner talk was interrupted when Tanis softly spoke in her musical language, "We need some help from you Hailey."

Hailey turned to look at the girl sitting next to her and wondered why they weren't better friends. Tanis was so nice and such a pretty girl. Hailey felt like she really wanted to help Tanis.

"How can I help you?"

"I've been looking for my Power Ring. Have you seen it?" asked Tanis.

"You have a Power Ring! I have one too. It's golden with a blue crystal in the center," offered Hailey.

"That sounds just like the one I lost. May I please see your ring?" asked Tanis expectantly.

"Um, sure," said Hailey slowly. "It's right here." Hailey pulled her Power Ring from her pocket and handed it to Tanis.

"That's just like mine!" exclaimed Tanis. "In fact, I'm sure this one is mine. You must have left yours at home."

Hailey had a puzzled look on her face as she thought about where she might have left her Power Ring.

"You might be right. I probably left mine at home. You should keep your Power Ring and I will look for mine when I get home."

"Thank you, Hailey. You have been extremely helpful," praised Tanis.

"Hailey, there is one more thing."

She tuned to look across the table at Damian.

"When the lunch bell rings, you will wake up and not remember any of our conversation. You will forget that you ever had a Power Ring. We were never here. You only had lunch with Mallory," insisted Damian in a quiet and forceful voice.

The twins got up smiling at each other, delighted with their cunning power of words.

"It's so much fun to have power over others," whispered Tanis giggling. "When Rebulus made us human, that was wonderful. But using our language to hypnotize those girls is pretty cool too!"

When the bell rang, Hailey looked up at Mallory and then at their half-eaten lunches. Hailey was confused. She was having difficulty focusing her eyes and her mind seemed fuzzy. It felt like a fog was just beginning to lift.

"What happened?" asked Hailey.

"I don't know. There must be something wrong with the school bells. We just sat down. I haven't finished my lunch and neither have you."

Hailey looked at her watch which confirmed the school bell was correct. Something was definitely wrong, but it wasn't the bell. She was rarely this confused, and it bothered her. The girls headed back to class eating their sandwiches as they walked.

"Mallory, can you take Lucas his homework today? I have to go home to find something I lost."

"Okay. I'll get the assignments from Miss Harrison after school. What did you lose?

"That's what's so strange. I'm not sure what I lost. I guess I'll remember when I get home," sighed Hailey.

The rest of the afternoon Hailey had trouble focusing on schoolwork and was glad when the bell finally rang. She hurried home after school hoping she could remember what she lost when she got to her room.

☼ ☼ ☼

"Hi Mom, I'm home."

"Hi sweetie, how was school? Did you learn anything new today?"

"I learned that I am forgetful, and I lose things. All afternoon I kept thinking I lost something, something important. But I can't remember what it might be."

"Did you lose it at school or at home?"

"That's the problem. I don't know what it was or where I lost it."

Hailey's mother could see she was distressed, and it wouldn't take much before Hailey would start crying. "Did you talk to Lucas about it?"

"No, he wasn't at school today. But maybe if I call him, I'll remember."

Hailey took the portable phone into her room and sat down on the bed. Neko, her Siamese cat, looked up sleepily from the windowsill then jumped to the bed next to Hailey. The cat stared at Hailey as if he were waiting for her to say something. Then, without warning, Neko looked around the room nervously and arched his back. Hailey could see the hair on his back stand up as he let out a low growl.

"What's wrong kitty? Who's here?"

Neko meowed loudly and ran out of the room.

Hailey shook her head and picked up the phone and called Lucas.

"Hey Hailey, thanks. Mallory just dropped off my homework. Why did you call on the phone?"

"Because I wanted to talk with you about something. Why else would I call?"

"No, I mean, why did you use the phone and not mental telepathy with your Power Ring."

"Power Ring? I don't have a Power Ring," answered Hailey.

"Stop teasing, Hailey?"

"I'm not teasing you. What are you talking about?"

"Hailey, are you serious? You really don't remember that you have a Power Ring! Prescott gave you a golden Power Ring with a blue crystal in the center. You and I each have a Power Ring and we use it for mental telepathy so we can talk with each other."

Snippets of Hailey's memory were beginning to return. She felt like she had a puzzle to solve, but there were too many pieces missing and there was no picture to see what the finished puzzle should look like. Tears were filling her eyes as the seriousness of the situation washed over her.

"Lucas," sobbed Hailey, "I think I lost the Power Ring!"

"How? Where? When did it happen?"

"I don't know, Lucas! I don't remember anything!" cried Hailey.

"Don't go anywhere," declared Lucas. "I'm coming over right now!"

Eighteen

A Very Sad Movie

*Those who ask the question
cannot avoid the answer.*

Tanis and Damian were excited to show Rebulus the prize they had gotten from Hailey. They found Rebulus waiting for them when they came home from school. This home was just a temporary place, but Tanis hoped it would be permanent in a few days. Maybe they would even find some real parents to adopt them.

Rebulus was such a strange creature. His eyes started twitching and Tanis knew he was going to say something about Lucas as she handed the Power Ring to him.

"Congratulations," offered Rebulus in his gravelly voice. "You have done well my children, but your task is not yet complete. You have but three days to get the Power Ring from Lucas."

Tanis had forgotten just how ugly this short harry creature was who squatted in front of them. She remembered the day he had turned her into a beautiful girl. She loved being a girl and had no intention of ever going back to the cave. She was anxious to be free of the deal they had made with *"Shorty"* and remain as a human forever.

She also felt a twinge of guilt for what they did to Hailey. It was kind of lonely having only a brother to whom she could talk. She wondered what it might be like to have girlfriends and to do things with them. Rebulus interrupted her fantasy.

"Hailey may have been an easy target," cautioned Rebulus. "Don't underestimate Lucas. He grows stronger and he has that old lizard with him. There's been a change of plans."

"Wait a minute!" protested Tanis. "You can't change our agreement. You said we get to remain human when we bring you Lucas's Power Ring."

"The part of remaining human has not changed. I just want something different."

"What do you want now?" questioned Damian, cautious and annoyed.

"I have a spy on the Light Bearer Council who is friendly to my cause. We know that Lucas has come into possession of the Sun Stone."

"The Sun Stone?" asked Tanis.

"Yes. It was hidden many years ago and only a few on the council knew its location. The keys to unlock the location of the Sun Stone were sent all over the earth to other Light Bearers so no single person possessed all the keys until now. Traveling with my spy, we followed Lucas to

Thailand and tried to stop him, but Lucas has strong friends. Well, I have strong friends too," growled Rebulus.

"What is the Sun Stone," asked Damian.

"It's a golden stone set in the most powerful of all Power Rings. I want the Sun Stone *and* the Fire Crystal," demanded Rebulus.

"That was not part of our agreement!" shouted Damian.

Rebulus glared at the twins as anger flashed in his red eyes. Then with a twisted smiled, he calmly threatened, "You see my little snakes, I set the rules and I can change them as I desire. If you can't do what I ask, I will find another and you two will be slithering on the ground in no time."

The twins looked at each other with a silent communication knowing they had to make a choice. Tanis knew what she wanted and reluctantly asked, "What do we need to do?"

☼ ☼ ☼

Lucas explained to his mom that Hailey had lost her Power Ring and he wanted to help her find it. His mom agreed and Lucas rushed over to Hailey's house on his bike. He knocked on Hailey's front door soon after he had hung up the phone.

"Hello Lucas," welcomed Mrs. Sinclair. "I heard you were sick today."

"I'm feeling better. Is Hailey here?"

"I'm here," said Hailey as she came up from behind her mom. "We're going to be in the backyard, Mom."

Hailey led the way to the chairs by the pool and the friends sat facing each other. Lucas could see her eyes were still red from crying and thought about the time that Hailey was so supportive and helpful when Senka stole his Power Ring.

"I know you must feel awful about losing your Power Ring. Do you have any idea what happened or where you lost it?"

"I don't know. I can't remember where I last had it or used it," replied Hailey.

"I know you had it at school this morning because you used it to ask me why I was at home."

"That's right. I remember now."

"Did you use it after you talked to me?"

"I don't think so," said Hailey as she struggled to remember anything. "My head feels kind of numb like my mouth does when I leave the dentist's office. It's so hard to think."

"Did you eat lunch with anyone?"

"Just Mallory. We sat at one of the tables by the grass."

"Was Damian or Tanis there?" questioned Lucas. He remembered when Hailey shifted into Mallory and met the twins in the library. The main thing Lucas learned was that the twins were not to be trusted.

"No, it was just Mallory and me. There was something extremely strange though. When the bell rang, after thirty minutes, we had hardly eaten any of our lunch. Everything was so foggy after that. Do you think Damian or Tanis had anything to do with how strange I'm feeling?"

"I don't know, but I may have a way to find out."

"How?" asked Hailey.

"Intelligence," said Lucas. He pulled his Power Ring from his pocket and turned it to the circle within a circle. He stood up as tall as he could, looked up to access the intelligence that was all around him. He squeezed the crystal and the vibration from the ring responded immediately.

Lucas quietly asked the unseen intelligence, "Where is Hailey's Power Ring?"

Tiny sparkling points of light began swirling around his head. As they came closer, they began striking his head. He felt a pleasant sensation when each of the tiny stars landed on him. Lucas closed his eyes, raised his hand above his head and thought about being open and receptive to any inspiration. Almost instantly, he saw something like a grainy old black and white movie in his mind. He saw Hailey and Mallory sitting at the lunch table. The more he focused, the movie transformed into color.

"What do you see?" asked Hailey nervously.

"I see you and Mallory are sitting at the table. Tanis and Damian walk up and sit down. You're having a conversation about a book, I think. Tanis is now speaking in a soft voice, but I cannot understand the words, but you and Mallory have a strange look, like you are in a trance. Hailey! I bet they hypnotized you both!"

"What about the Power Ring?"

"You seem to be smiling. No, wait! Now you look confused. You stand up and pull your Power Ring out of your pocket."

This was just a movie in his head, but Lucas was still frustrated because he couldn't do anything to stop Tanis.

"Now you're handing Tanis your Power Ring. The twins talk to you some more and then I see them smiling as they walk away." Lucas felt helpless as the pictures in his mind started fading.

"Is that it?" questioned Hailey. "I can't believe I gave Tanis my Power Ring! There's no way I would have done that unless I *was* hypnotized!"

Lucas had to get over the feeling of helplessness. He was a Light Bearer, and he had some awesome powers. He just needed to ask himself the right questions.

"You need to trust me. I will take care of this problem. I will get your Power Ring back," assured Lucas, even though he didn't know how.

"What are you going to do?"

"I'm not sure yet, but if I talk with Prescott, I'm certain I'll find a solution."

"If you decide to talk with Damian or Tanis, please, please be careful. If they had some hypnotic power over me, they might try the same thing on you and take your Power Ring. Call if you need my help. But I guess you'll have to use a phone," said Hailey with a weak smile.

"Oh, right," said Lucas. "Okay, I'll call you on the phone or come to your house. See you at school tomorrow. And don't feel so bad, This helps us understand what we are up against."

After Lucas left, Hailey went back to her room and wrote a letter to Tanis. Maybe, just maybe she could find a way to change her mind and return the Power Ring.

Nineteen

Leap of Faith in Time

Knowledge shines light to the darkness.

Lucas left Hailey's house and rode his bike to the street where the twins lived. He hid his bike in the bushes on the corner and considered his next move. Lucas was glad the intelligence had helped him to see the "movie" with Tanis and Damian sitting at the lunch table with the girls. He knew with absolute certainty that the twins were involved in the disappearance of Hailey's ring.

"Lucas, what are you planning to do?"

He was not surprised to hear Prescott in his mind. In fact, he liked it. Prescott always seemed to know where he was and what he was doing. He felt a little safer because Prescott seemed to know when Lucas needed him.

"I'm going to prove that Tanis and Damian are the ones who stole Hailey's Power Ring."

"Why do you think they stole it?" asked Prescott.

"Why? Somehow, they must be working with Rebulus or maybe they're controlled by him. But

Prescott, what Hailey told me about what happened at lunch and the things I saw in my mind are different. Why is that?"

"Lucas, the more you use the Power Ring and the power of intelligence, the more likely you will get ideas and impressions of the truth," shared Prescott. "Just because you cannot see something with your eyes, is no proof that it does not exist. The truth will come as thoughts or pictures into your mind."

"That's exactly what happened to me. Hailey told me one thing and I saw something different in my mind," revealed Lucas.

"I am sure she was telling you what SHE thought was the truth," assured Prescott. "We may be told something that is believed to be a hard fact, when in reality, it is false. But, if it is shown in such a convincing way, we believe what we are told or shown. If you are sure about going to the twin's house, you must be very cautious my friend."

"Prescott, do you think Rebulus is controlling the twins?"

"I am quite certain of it. That is why you must be careful," warned Prescott. "Rebulus has been trying to steal your light and the Power Ring. Senka failed and now he may have convinced the twins to help him. But there is something else that is concerning me."

"What is it?" asked Lucas.

"I believe there is someone controlling Rebulus," cautioned Prescott. "I believe it is a Light

Bearer who wants to take the Sun Stone from you. If I am right, it is someone who is much stronger than you."

"Should I wait for you to be with me when I talk with the twins?" asked Lucas.

"No, but I will be there if you need help. Remember, I see what you see."

"Prescott, before I go to their house, I have a question about the Power Ring."

"What do you want to know?" responded Prescott.

"I know I can use the powers individually, but is it possible to use more than one power at the same time?"

"I was wondering when you would ask that question. You are growing in your ability and confidence. Lucas, the Power Ring belongs to you, and it will respond to your thoughts. You may indeed use more than one power at the same time. In fact, you can use as many powers as you need at the same time."

That was the answer Lucas wanted. To test his plan, Lucas turned the pointer to become invisible and squeezed the crystal. He disappeared immediately and came out from behind the bushes. Believing he would remain unseen; he turned the pointer to telekinesis and focused on floating like he did during the fire at school when he saved Anna. Lucas started gliding unseen down the sidewalk toward the house where the twins lived. An older boy at school was coming down the sidewalk on his skateboard and rode right past Lucas as if he wasn't there.

"*Cool!*" thought Lucas as he considered his new skill while approaching the twins' home. Lucas wished he had x-ray vision and the power to see through walls, but for now, he just listened carefully for any sounds. He silently floated up to the porch and listened. The front door was open, and he heard a conversation though the screen door. Lucas was surprised to hear Damian yelling and wondered who was on the receiving end of his anger.

"We know there are only two days left! We gave you Hailey's Power Ring! Isn't that enough to work your dark magic?"

Lucas recognized the raspy voice he heard next. It was a low voice but filled with anger as it emphasized each word.

"You both knew who I was when you agreed to my terms. I said I wanted Lucas's Power Ring, and you brought me Hailey's. You have only two days to bring me Lucas's Power Ring. If not, you become snakes again."

"*Snakes again!*" Lucas could not believe what he heard! Is it possible that Tanis and Damian really were snakes?

"If you fail me, you will be slithering once again on the cold rocks of the cavern where I found you," snarled Rebulus.

After some silence, there was a noticeable change in his tone when Rebulus asked, "Does Lucas know where you live?"

"How should I know?" replied Damian impatiently.

"Why does it matter?" questioned Tanis.

"It matters because all of my senses tell me that a Light Bearer is near and also because my eye is twitching."

Lucas let out an audible gasp.

"What was that?" asked Rebulus sharply.

"I didn't hear anything," said Tanis.

"Go find him! I know he's here," demanded Rebulus.

"Who's here?" asked Tanis.

"Lucas Lightfoot, that's who! I can sense he's nearby," replied Rebulus angrily.

Lucas held his breath and remained motionless. All he could hear for a few moments was the blood pounding in his ears. Knowing he was invisible, he willed himself to be calm when he heard Prescott again.

"Lucas, do you need my help?"

"I do. I think Tanis and Damian are snakes who have somehow been changed by Rebulus to become human. They just admitted to taking the ring from Hailey and they have given it to Rebulus. They now want to steal my ring. What do I do? How can I get into the house without them knowing and get Hailey's ring back?"

Prescott replied thoughtfully, *"They say they have the ring, but what if they did not have the ring?"*

"But they do have it," replied Lucas.

"But... what if they never got the Power Ring from Hailey in the first place? Now that you know, is there anything you can do to prevent them from stealing the ring?"

Lucas considered what Prescott might be suggesting and realized there might be a way to prevent Tanis and Damian from ever getting the Power Ring at the lunch table today.

"Thanks, Prescott. You've given me an idea."

Lucas heard footsteps running toward the front door and the screen door flew open. Lucas backed away just in time but felt the gust of air as the screen swung by just inches from his face. Lucas held his breath as Damian stood on the porch looking up and down the street. Confident he had not been seen, Lucas hurried back to his bike and rode home. He rushed to his room to discuss his plan with Prescott.

"Prescott, what if I go back in time and sit with Hailey and Mallory to see what Tanis and Damian do to steal Hailey's ring?"

"If they were able to get Hailey's Power Ring, might they also be able to take yours as well?" suggested Prescott.

"But I can be there and prevent it," insisted Lucas. "I'm sure of it!"

"Do not rush too quickly into what might be a trap. I suggest you make yourself invisible and

stay a good distance away and observe," cautioned Prescott. *"If Hailey was hypnotized, you could be as well. I recommend you plan very carefully how you can use time to your advantage."*

Lucas could not imagine how the twins could trap him, but he agreed, "Okay. I'll think about it. And yes, I'll hang back and watch closely."

☼ ☼ ☼

The next morning Lucas was feeling good about his plan to stop Damian and Tanis. Lucas realized he didn't need to get the Power Ring back from the twins, he only had to prevent it from ever being taken. Lucas knew the school well and selected a location on the backside of the school where he would not be seen. He turned the pointer to the triangle with the circle on top to jump through time. He imagined the location he wanted to be at exactly 11:40, a few minutes before the lunch bell rang and squeezed the crystal on his Power Ring. Instantly, he was transported back to yesterday. He made himself invisible and walked over to a place on the blacktop where he could see, but not hear Damian. Hailey and Mallory walked out to the lunch table and sat down. Tanis and Damian follow behind them a minute later. From a distance, he saw both Tanis and Damian talking to the girls. As Lucas watched, there was something extremely odd about the appearance of both Hailey and Mallory. It was as though they were being hypnotized, just like he had seen in the movie in his mind.

He couldn't risk walking over to the twins knowing they wanted his Power Ring as well. He looked for the way to distract Damian and saw a possible solution. Lucas often played soccer with Gavin and Braxton, two boys from Ms. Stephens class. They were accomplished soccer players and had taught Lucas how to kick the ball hard and straight.

Today they were in the field near the lunch tables with five other boys kicking the ball around. Still invisible, Lucas ran into the middle of the group. Braxton had kicked a low rolling ball and Lucas rushed in and gave the soccer ball a mighty kick toward Damian's back. Adding a little telekinesis to guide the ball, it struck Damian right in the middle of his back where Lucas had imagined a target. Damian jumped up and angrily yelled at Braxton, the closest boy. The soccer ball had done the trick and Hailey and Mallory were shaking their heads looking confused. Lucas ran back to the office building, became visible and came around the corner of the building and yelled.

"Hailey Sinclair, you're wanted in the school office. There's an emergency!"

Damian and Tanis gave Lucas a look that was full of anger. He was close enough, though, to see their eyes flash yellow like the snakes they were.

"I'd better go see what the emergency is," said Hailey as she wrapped her uneaten sandwich and stuffed it in her lunch sack.

Hailey ran over to Lucas and said, "What's wrong? What's the emergency?"

"Come with me," said Lucas urgently. As they hurried around the corner of the building out of view of the twins, Lucas excitedly explained, "Tanis and Damian are snakes working for Rebulus who changed them into humans, and they plan to steal your Power Ring today."

"Wait, what? Slow down! How's that possible?" questioned Hailey. "Why do you think they are snakes and how do you know what they're planning? Wait, I thought you were at home sick today!"

"I know this sounds strange, but after I found out what they did today, I secretly went to their house and heard them talking to Rebulus. That's when I found out they were snakes. I thought about it overnight then got up tomorrow morning and jumped back in time to today to warn you they are going to steal your Power Ring during lunch. It looks like they were trying to hypnotize you and convince you to give Tanis your Power Ring. Is that clear?"

"Well, not really," said Hailey somewhat confused. She put her hands to her temples trying to remember the last ten minutes and said, "Just before Damian was hit in his back with the soccer ball, I was listening to their strange language. It was very soothing, almost like music, and that may be how they were trying to hypnotize me."

"Whatever it was, it seemed to be working," said Lucas. "You and Mallory both looked like you were in a daze."

"Well, it's a good thing that Damian was hit with the soccer ball," marveled Hailey." When she saw Lucas grinning, she asked, "Was that you? That was you! You kicked the soccer into Damian's back!"

"At your service," said Lucas with a smile.

"Well, thank you. I can't believe they're really snakes," said Hailey. "I guess Rebulus has a lot more power than we thought."

"I better get back to tomorrow because I'm home sick today," laughed Lucas. "Just be careful this afternoon."

"I will," assured Hailey. "Do you think I should give you my Power Ring in case they try something else?"

"That's an excellent idea," replied Lucas. "You can pick it up later."

Lucas smiled as he disappeared. Hailey threw away her sandwich and ate her apple as she thoughtfully walked back to class as she considered the blessing and burden of the Power Ring.

☼ ☼ ☼

After Mallory had walked back to class, Damian and Tanis remained at the table.

"I'm sure Lucas was somehow behind that soccer ball! He really destroyed our plans today," exclaimed Damian in rage

"We only have two days left. What are we going to do?" asked Tanis.

"I heard Rebulus talking with someone he called the Storm Maker. Maybe we can get some help from him," suggested Damian.

Twenty

Stormy Weather

You may not be able to change the situation, but you can change how you choose to deal with it.

Realizing just how dangerous Rebulus and the twins were, Lucas asked Prescott what they could do to protect themselves. Lucas was surprised when Prescott suggested he talk with Katrina and Grandpa Jack, who was visiting her home. Katrina lived almost two miles away on the other side of Canyon Park. When they left Hailey's home, the sky was blue with just a slight breeze. By the time they had walked to the park, the sky had become dark and threatening. Yet, Lucas knew that the weather forecast was supposed to be sunny all day. It just didn't feel right.

"Who do you think started this storm?" asked Lucas as pulled his baseball cap tighter on his head. Hailey's hair was flying in all directions, so she grabbed her hair and quickly pulled it up in a ponytail.

"What do you mean, 'who?'"

"There's not supposed to be a storm or even clouds today. It kind of feels like the storm we had in Thailand with Andy. Someone was trying to block the sun there and maybe someone is trying to stop us from getting to Katrina's house now."

"Do you think it's Rebulus?"

"I don't think so. He's been trying to get our Power Rings by using the twins. Prescott told me he thinks there's someone with more power who's behind Rebulus, maybe even a Light Bearer."

"Wait, what? Aren't Light Bearers supposed to do good?" questioned Hailey.

"They are," replied Lucas. "But there might be one who has let anger and pride rule their actions in order to have more power."

Lucas felt his ears pop as the pressure dropped. They were walking right into a cold wind that was kicking up a lot of dust.

"Look at that!" exclaimed Hailey as she pointed to the clouds in front of them.

Lucas looked up see a dark funnel cloud coming down toward the ground. "We never have tornados in Southern California," shouted Lucas.

The wind started getting stronger as dust, leaves and trash began blowing directly at them. The wind was deafening as the funnel cloud moved dangerously toward them.

"We'd better get home while we can," yelled Lucas. "We can't go through the park anymore. The wind's too strong!"

"If you're right and there is someone trying to get to us, there's no time to get back home. I have a better idea," yelled Hailey.

They were leaning into the wind and about to be blown away when they grabbed onto the trunk of a tree that was close by. Hailey quickly pulled out her Power Ring and turned the pointer to the cloud symbol to control the weather. She had one arm around the tree and was struggling to squeeze the crystal. Lucas held on to a large branch but lost his footing as his legs were blown out from underneath him. He watched as Hailey closed her eyes and clenched her teeth in desperation. They were being hit by flying trash and branches picked up by the dark cloud of the mini tornado. Suddenly, a hailstorm began with small hail stones bouncing all around them. The trees offered little protection, as they were still being stung by the torrent of hail stones.

"Hailey, you can do this!" encouraged Lucas in his mind.

Within moments, a powerful gust of warm air came rushing down from the hills above the park and pushed back against the tornado. The tornado began breaking up and dissolving. The dark cloud covering the park thinned out and the sunshine broke through.

"You did it Hailey! Let's go. I think we can make it to Katrina's house now."

As they continued running through the park, suddenly, they heard a loud whooshing sound and the loud boom of thunder. The tornado took shape again. This time there were lightning flashes all around them, blocking their escape.

"Someone knows we're here and is trying to prevent us from leaving. Let's run for that spot under the rock formation. It should protect us from the hail and lightning," yelled Lucas as he pointed to a rock.

They dashed to the opening in the rock and turned to see the hail stones, now the size of golf balls, crashing through the trees and knocking off branches.

"Hailey, let's try something else," as Lucas pointed to the double "T" with the dot above it on his Power Ring.

Hailey nodded her head in agreement. They both concentrated on the power of stopping time while squeezing the crystal on their Power Rings.

"Look at that!" said Lucas. "It's working!"

They were amazed to see the air filled with white hail stones frozen and floating in mid-air. It was incredibly beautiful despite the destructive force of the hailstorm. Looking through the hail stones, they saw the tree they had just been grasping moments ago. Lightning had hit the tree, splitting it in half. Amazingly, the bolt of lightning, some thirty feet away, was frozen in time as it hit the tree. Even though the lightning was motionless, they could still feel the extreme heat that came from the lightning bolt.

"It's fortunate we weren't hit with lightning while holding on to that tree," said Hailey.

"Hailey, who do you see in the park?" asked Lucas. They both looked out from the protection of the rock at the park.

"There's no one," answered Hailey.

"That's right," said Lucas. "On Saturday afternoon, this park is usually crowded."

"Oh yeah! Something is definitely not right. We need to get out of here, Lucas," urged Hailey. "I have a really bad feeling about this storm."

"I agree. We need to go."

They stepped out into the motionless hailstorm and started pushing aside the ice crystals that were in their way. They picked up speed and started walking faster. Suddenly, the hail stones rose upward into the sky. Up, up, up they went.

"Hailey, are you doing that?

"No, it's not me. What's happening?"

"I think there's someone with stronger powers than both of us."

They watched the hail stones rising in the air and tried to imagine what would happen if they all came down at once.

"Lucas, what should we do?"

"*Prescott, we need help! Someone is trying to stop us from leaving the park and getting to Katrina's house. Prescott! Prescott! Can you hear me?*"

"What's wrong? Why isn't Prescott answering?"

"I don't know, I don't know," stammered Lucas.

"There must be a way through this storm," said Hailey hopefully.

"That's it!" exclaimed Lucas. "We'll use the power of telekinesis and push away anything that can hit us. If we run, we can get to Katrina's in just a few minutes. Are you ready?"

Hailey nodded and they set their Power Rings to the three arrows. They briefly looked at each other for encouragement and took a deep breath.

"All right, let's go."

As they started running, the hail stones stopped moving upward, paused slightly, and then came speeding earthward. Lucas and Hailey used their telekinesis power and created an open path, almost like a tunnel free of hail stones.

"We're almost there," said Lucas. "I see her house!"

Surprisingly, the earth split apart in front of them and opened like a huge mouth, creating a massive opening in the grass. Hailey and Lucas tumbled down the open throat of the earth and everything went dark.

Twenty-One

Sun Stone and Light Power

There is no darkness so dense, so menacing, or so difficult that cannot be overcome by light.

"Welcome to my sanctuary, boy," sneered the gravelly voice.

Lucas opened his eyes, but he had trouble focusing. The back of his head was throbbing as he struggled to sit up on the cold rocky ground. He had trouble figuring out where he was and how he got here. He reached around to feel the source of his aching head and found a "goose egg" on the back of his head.

As his eyes adjusted to his surroundings, he appeared to be in a large cavern. It was about the height of a two-story house inside with rock formations scattered around the ground. One wall had a stream of water trickling down into a large pool. Lucas saw an opening in the rock about thirty feet above the ground. He caught a glimpse of blue sky and wondered if there was a Light Bearer up there who could rescue him. The light filtered down from the natural skylight and Lucas saw a possible escape tunnel at each end of the cavern. The

gravelly voice was unmistakable. Somehow Rebulus had brought him here, but he had no memory of how it happened.

"Sorry about the head," said Rebulus without any compassion in his voice. "You fell and there was no one to catch you. It seems that all the other Light Bearers have deserted you."

Lucas knew that would never happen and guessed Rebulus was messing with his mind. He touched his pants pocket to feel for his Power Ring hoping to use it to free himself.

"Hello Lucas. It's so good of you to join us. Are you looking for this?"

Lucas knew that voice as well. It was Damian and he was holding the Power Ring that Prescott had given Lucas, but the fire crystal was missing and in its place was a black stone.

"I knew you were no good," snapped Lucas. "How could you sink so low as to be on the same side as this evil creature?"

"Quite the opposite," replied Damian. "As a snake, I was already slithering low on the ground and Rebulus gave me legs to stand. Now I'm just like you and I plan to do whatever it takes to stay this way. I think he did a rather fine job of making me human, don't you?"

Slowly emphasizing each word, Lucas looked Damian in the eye, scolding him, "You... are... nothing... like... me!"

Lucas was ready to tell Damian what he really thought, when he saw Tanis come out of the shadows behind her brother. Lucas wanted to scold her also for being a part of this when he saw the sadness in her face. Lucas had a clear impression that even though Tanis may have gone along with this kidnapping, she wasn't happy about it. Maybe he could use her to help escape.

"You might be wondering why you are here as my guest," mused Rebulus.

"I don't feel much like a guest, with my feet tied up," replied Lucas. "Is this how you treat all your guests?"

"Only our special guests, like Light Bearers," chuckled Rebulus.

"What am I doing here?" demanded Lucas.

"Fine, no pleasant conversation, let's get down to business," said Rebulus. "I already have both of your Power Rings and I will find a use for them."

"*Power Rings, does he have mine and Hailey's too?*" thought Lucas.

"I may even give them to Damian and Tanis for helping me. I won't need them when you give me the Sun Stone."

"And why would I do that?" asked Lucas boldly.

"Because you wouldn't want anything terrible to happen to your friend," cautioned Rebulus as he pointed to a figure behind him lying in a corner of the cave.

Lucas turned to look over his right shoulder and saw Hailey lying on her side with her back against a rock.

"Hailey!" shouted Lucas. "Are you okay?"

Hailey started groaning as she pushed herself into a sitting position. Lucas was beginning to remember running across the park with Hailey when the ground opened and swallowed them.

"What happened?" asked Hailey.

"Hailey! Hailey, are you hurt?" asked Lucas as he tried to stand. He forgot his feet were tied and landed on his shoulder with a thud.

"I think I'm okay," mumbled Hailey. "Where are we?"

"You're a guest in my home," replied Rebulus.

Lucas turned his head and shot an angry stare toward Rebulus.

"In fact, you will be my guest until Lucas brings me the Sun Stone."

Hailey looked up in surprise at Rebulus and the twins. She caught Tanis's eye and gave her a pleading look. Tanis turned her head and looked away.

Lucas felt his shoulder and neck muscles tightening and his legs started to shake as he experienced a flood of emotions. It was a jumble of anger, hate and fear all bottled up ready to explode. He wasn't so much afraid for himself, but he was very concerned about Hailey's safety.

"Here's what you're going to do, Lucas," demanded Rebulus. "You are going to go get the Sun Stone and bring it back to me and I will let you and Hailey return to your homes, but you will be weak without your Power Rings."

"Why would I trust anything you say," countered Lucas as he considered his escape options. He wondered which Light Bearer he could get to help when another figure stepped out of the shadows. He was a tall man wearing a hat that kept his face hidden. As the stranger neared, Lucas saw the wide moustache. It was Alastair Janus with the nose-hair moustache!

"Hello lad," greeted Alastair with his deep British accent. "You have my word as a gentleman and a Light Bearer, you and Hailey will go free."

"Do you really expect me to believe you?" answered Lucas skeptically.

Lucas knew Alastair was lying when he leaned back, crossed his arms, and looked at Lucas with annoyance. Lucas had the birthright, and he was sure Alastair knew that as well.

"How is it possible that someone on the Light Bearer Council is here with Rebulus?" asked Lucas to no one in particular, but just to make a point. Then he remembered seeing Alastair at the bus stop with Senka.

"What? No 'Hello, how are you?'" asked Alastair. "I haven't seen you since you and Hailey visited me at Stonehenge. Did you enjoy your trip to England? It really is a beautiful country. Don't you agree?"

Lucas said nothing and just shook his head.

"Well maybe you can offer me an apology," said Alastair.

"For what? Why would I owe you an apology?" asked Lucas making no effort to conceal his disgust.

"For trying to kill my daughter, Senka."

"I didn't kill her!" snapped Lucas. "It was the river. The flash flood was responsible for her death, not me. She was in the wrong place at the wrong time. The beast that died in the flood wasn't your daughter, it was a wolf."

"Or so you say, but I raised her like a daughter. She was a brilliant student and learned much from me. She volunteered to help Rebulus, and I agreed. Unfortunately, she saw you as an easy target. And that's a mistake I shall NOT make."

Alastair kept his composure like an English gentleman, but Lucas could sense a deep anger that wrapped itself around each word Alastair spoke. When he met Alastair at Stonehenge, Lucas knew there was something not right with him. He remembered Megan saying that 'Alastair was off his trolley.' She sure got that right. Although he was on the Light Bearer Council, he was not like the others.

"Okay laddie, there's no apology. Well then, you will go to your home, retrieve the Sun Stone, and bring it back here to me. I saw the look on your face when you were considering which Light Bearer to bring back with you. There will be none. Do you understand? If you fail to follow my instructions, I am quite sure Hailey's parents will really miss their young lassie and *you* will be to blame. To make sure there is no deviation from my plan, Damian will go with you, and he will bring back the Sun Stone."

Lucas was wondering how Alastair knew the Sun Stone was at his home when Damian walked over to Lucas and pulled something from his pocket. With a flick of the wrist, the gleaming silver blade snapped out of the knife handle and Hailey let out a loud gasp.

Damian came at Lucas with the knife and Hailey screamed, "Stop!" and all eyes turned to her.

"Stop what?" questioned Damian. He then stooped down and easily cut through the rope tied around Lucas's legs like it was string.

"Get up Lucas, we're going to get the Sun Stone."

Lucas looked over at Hailey and gave her a weak smile. She smiled back and silently mouthed the words, *"I trust you,"* as she nodded her head.

If only he could read her mind to know if she had some idea for an escape plan so they could work together. He was feeling the gravity of the situation when he felt a hand shove him from behind.

Damian turned on a flashlight and said, "This way Lucas," as he pointed the beam of light in the direction of a tunnel. One more shove from behind and he started walking slowly in the direction of the circle of light bouncing on the ground in front of him.

☼ ☼ ☼

Using the power of mental telepathy, Prescott called out to all the Master Light Bearers. *"Does anyone know where Lucas and Hailey are? I have been trying to contact them, but they do not answer."*

Each Light Bearer responded they did not know. All of them replied, except Alastair Janus which confirmed to Prescott who the traitor was.

"We will find Hailey and my grandson," assured Jackson. *"I am visiting with Katrina, and she says she has many friends who can look for the kids."*

"That is good," replied Prescott. *"I am concerned that one of our own is behind their disappearance.*

Lucas has become strong, but I believe he is up against a dangerous threat with Alastair."

"*That confirms my suspicions,*" replied Jackson. "*I saw the clues but didn't want to believe it.*"

Katrina stepped out into the back yard which overlooked a woodland park. She called out to the animals that lived in the trees, the brush and in the ground. Within a few minutes, there were birds, squirrels, skunks, foxes, and a couple of mountain lions.

"My dear friends, thank you for coming to help! Two young Light Bearers are missing. We need your help to find them," pleaded Katrina. "Hailey and Lucas are ten years old. We believe they have been kidnapped and are being held against their will."

Jackson added, "Not only is Lucas my grandson, but he has the birthright to lead all Light Bearers one day and must be protected."

The animals began to anxiously chatter among themselves. One of the Red Crowned parrots flew to the fountain beside Katrina.

"I know them," squawked the parrot. "We helped return a special ring to the boy and girl. Not long ago, I saw two boys walking in the creek. One of them was Lucas. They had come out of a tunnel in the creek bank near his house.

"There are a lot of holes near the creek and tunnels under the city," offered one of the skunks. "We know all the underground passages around here. We may be small, but we are many and can help."

"Prescott, did you hear all of that," asked Jackson.

"I did and I may know why they are coming here to Lucas's home. I believe Lucas is being forced by Alastair to give him the Sun Stone. They might be holding Hailey to make sure Lucas returns with it," replied Prescott. *"Somehow Alastair has found a way to block Lucas from my thoughts."*

"We will have the parrot take us to the opening in the creek," said Jackson.

"I will meet you there," assured Prescott.

☼ ☼ ☼

Lucas led the way through the maze of tunnels with Damian close behind directing him with the flashlight. Sometimes he had to duck to avoid tree roots and brushed away cobwebs. As they turned a corner, Lucas saw the light from outside.

"Don't get any ideas about running. I have your Power Ring, but with the storm crystal, it only responds to me now."

When they stepped into the light, Lucas had to shade his eyes from the glare of the noon sun. He was surprised to see he was in the creek only a few houses from his own home. Lucas knew Prescott was there and he would help.

"Let's go to the bridge and we'll walk to your house from there," directed Damian. He put the flashlight in his pocket and said, "Move it, Lucas."

Lucas climbed up the bank out of the creek. He remembered meeting Kevin, the school bully, under the bridge. Damian was also a bully, but Lucas really preferred Kevin right now.

As they neared Lucas's house, Damian saw Mallory sitting on her porch across the street.

"Stop right here," commanded Damian. He removed the Power Ring from his pocket, turned the pointer and pressed against the black stone.

"There, that ought to keep things still until I get the Sun Stone. Keep moving."

Lucas looked at a motionless Mallory and saw her neighbor's sprinklers with water droplets frozen in midair. Damian had stopped time and Lucas wondered if anyone in his home would be frozen in time.

"Go on in," directed Damian. "I'm sure everything will be quiet inside your house."

Lucas found his mom in the kitchen making sandwiches. She was like a statue holding a piece of bread in one hand and spreading mayonnaise with a knife in the other hand. He saw the empty can of tuna fish on the counter. Normally the tuna fish had an unmistakable odor, but Lucas realized he couldn't smell anything. He knew that sound stopped but he never realized that smells also stopped. Lucas might have laughed at that thought, but nothing was funny right now.

"Where's the Sun Stone?" asked Damian.

"It's in my bedroom."

"Well, what are you waiting for? Let's go get it."

Lucas stopped to look in the family room where he saw Gavin and Madison frozen while playing a video game. They too were motionless, something he rarely saw. He wondered if he would ever see his family again. He wished he could talk with them, hug them, say goodbye to them and tell them he loved them. He saw Ranger looking in through the sliding glass door. His ears were back, and he was frozen in the middle of barking.

"Keep moving. I haven't got all day."

Lucas walked into his room and saw Prescott was also motionless. Still, he tried to contact him through his thoughts.

"Prescott, can you hear me?" pleaded Lucas.

No reply. Lucas realized he might be on his own. But he still had the Sun Stone. He had used it a few times to see what was possible and was surprised by its power. Without any specific markings, Lucas could choose any power he needed from the Sun Stone. He shuddered to think what that power could do in the hands of Rebulus or Alastair. Fortunately, the Sun Stone only responded to his thoughts, as least for now.

"Get the Sun Stone and hand it to me if you want to see Hailey again!"

Lucas walked to the bookcase and hesitated for a moment. He saw his seashell collection and thought back to when he went to the beach with Hailey and her family. They had found some rare and beautiful shells. He had to find a way to save

Hailey one more time. He removed the box that looked like an old leather-bound book from the bookcase. When he turned around, Damian grabbed the box and opened it to make sure the Sun Stone was inside. The blinding light of the stone filled the bedroom and caused Damian to fall backward in surprise, dropping the box.

"Put it back inside," yelled Damian as he covered his eyes to block the brilliant light.

Lucas picked up the miniature sun and placed it back into the box. He closed the cover and the room returned to normal as he set the box on the desk next to Prescott's cage.

"Now that I have the Sun Stone, I don't need you anymore," said Damian with confidence. He pulled out the Power Ring and pressed the black storm crystal. Immediately, Lucas flew up in the air as his head hit the ceiling with a thud.

"Wait!" cautioned Lucas. "Before you do anything you'll regret, are you sure you can carry the box?"

With Lucas glued to the ceiling above his bed, Damian reached for the box and a jolt of electricity jumped from the box to Damian's hand.

"Ow!" screamed Damian as sparks of electricity bounced all over his hand and up his arm. Immediately, he could smell the odor of burning hair. "What did you do?" shouted Damian.

"Why do you think I'm doing anything? I'm stuck on the ceiling, but I suggest you let me down.

You still need me to carry the box because only a Light Bearer can hold it."

Damian considered his options and decided that getting the Sun Stone to Rebulus and Alastair was the key to remaining human for Tanis and himself. Even if Lucas carried it, the Sun Stone, it would still get to the cavern. He let go of the storm crystal and Lucas dropped like a sandbag and landed on the bed. Lucas had the air knocked out of his lungs and heard the wooden bed frame crack.

"I guess that's why Mom doesn't want me jumping on my bed," thought Lucas. But that was the least of his worries.

He touched the back of his head and felt the warmth of fresh blood on the raised bump on his head. When he hit his head on the ceiling, the gash on his head opened. He grabbed a white sock from the floor and glared at Damian as he held the sock against his head to stop the bleeding.

"Pick up the Sun Stone. Rebulus is waiting for us to return. I'm sure Hailey is anxious to see you again too."

Lucas picked up the box with the treasure inside and placed it in his green shoulder pack. Damian had no idea that Lucas had learned to control the Sun Stone with his mind. Lucas could make it shine like the sun, shoot out bolts of lightning or become as cold as dry ice. As they headed for the door, Lucas felt something familiar. A feeling of relief flooded over Lucas as he realized his invisible friend was on his shoulder. As he stepped into the hall, he took a quick glance back in his room and smiled when he saw an empty cage.

Twenty-Two

In the Arms of an Angel

Sacrifice is the greatest expression of love.

Katrina and Jackson were still in her backyard deciding how to best rescue the children, when several of the skunks came scampering out of the woods to tell them where Lucas and Hailey were being held. Katrina thanked the skunks. With the Red Crowned parrot leading the way, Katrina and Jackson went quickly to the entrance of the tunnel Damian and Lucas had used. The parrot reported that the boys had gone to Lucas's home but had not yet returned. While they waited for the boys, they discussed what might come next.

"Do you have any idea why Alastair would do this?" asked Katrina.

"I imagine he's angry he wasn't selected to lead the council," replied Jackson. "Alastair knows that Lucas has the birthright and jealousy has clouded his judgment. He wants the ultimate power of the Sun Stone."

"Whatever the reason, Jackson, we must protect Lucas at all costs," replied Katrina solemnly.

They didn't have to wait very long before they heard Damian and Lucas come down the bank and walk along the creek.

"I think we should make ourselves invisible," said Jackson. With a nod of agreement from Katrina, the pair disappeared, and the faint remains of sparkling dust settled to the ground.

Lucas stopped at the entrance to the cave and looked around. He knew there were Light Bearers nearby. He could sense their presence. That's when he heard Prescott on his shoulder whisper to his mind.

"You have friends close by who will protect you. We will follow you into the cave."

"Stop looking around! There's no one coming for you!" declared Damian.

"I guess you're right," said Lucas with a sigh. As he turned to the cave entrance, he felt the invisible Prescott jump from his shoulder.

☼ ☼ ☼

Tanis smiled as she thought about some of the girls in Miss Harrison's class and wondered what it would be like to have girlfriends. She wished she could have friends to talk to and laugh with like she had seen other girls at school. She wondered if she could ever have what Hailey and Lucas had. It was more than friendship. It was a commitment to help and protect each other.

She also wondered if Rebulus was really going to keep his promise of letting her and Damian remain human. She needed to talk with Hailey. Tanis walked over to Rebulus and Alastair who were in a far corner of the cave angrily discussing something with low voices.

"Hailey looks thirsty. Can I give her some water?" asked Tanis.

"Certainly," said Alastair. "After all, she is our guest. But don't get too close to her."

Tanis went to her backpack and pulled out a bottle of water. She walked over to where Hailey was sitting and wondered what type of reaction she would get. Tanis knew she was being watched, so she made sure she kept her back to Rebulus.

"Would you like some water?" asked Tanis holding out the bottle.

Hailey looked at Tanis with suspicion, but slowly softened her expression wondering if she could turn Tanis from an enemy to a friend.

"I'm scared, uncomfortable and hurt," replied Hailey. "So yes, I would like some water," as she took the bottle from Tanis.

"Do you think Lucas will bring the Sun Stone so we can set you free?" asked Tanis softly.

"If he can, I'm sure he's going to try," whispered Hailey.

Since meeting Mrs. Moore, Hailey realized she was developing the ability to sense what other people were feeling and wondered if she was becoming an empath like the teacher. Hailey sensed there was a change in Tanis. It was a change for the better. She was beginning to act more human with compassion and not like a snake that acted purely on instinct.

"When you were unconscious, I was looking for your Power Ring and found a small envelope in your back pocket with my name on it," whispered Tanis.

"Did you read the letter inside the envelope?" asked Hailey. "Did anyone else see it?"

"Yes, I read it and no, no one else saw it," replied Tanis. "Did you really mean all those things you said?"

"Yes. I really thought we could have been friends if the situation were different," assured Hailey. "It seems like you aren't free to make any decisions on you own."

"I know. I gave up my freedom to choose after we made that deal with the little devil over there," whispered Tanis.

Tanis looked off into the distance with an empty stare. She let out a long sigh as sadness washed over her.

"I wish we were back in the classroom with the other kids. We really did have fun in class," confessed Tanis. "Tell Miss Harrison and the girls in the class that I really enjoyed being in school and I will miss them."

"Why? What do you mean?" asked Hailey.

"I don't think Rebulus is going to keep his promise. But Hailey, when he changed us from being snakes to become human, it was the most wonderful feeling I've ever had. It's so amazing to be a girl. I love it! I love having hands and feet and long hair I can brush and lovely clothes to wear. Damian and I love eating hamburgers and French fries. Oh, and we both love ice cream!" giggled Tanis excitedly.

"I also like long hair and nice clothes and being a girl," confided Hailey. "In fact, we like a lot of the same things."

Tanis had enjoyed a taste of what it must be like to have friends and wondered if she could help Hailey.

"What did Rebulus promise you?" asked Hailey quietly.

"He said we could remain human if we got the Power Rings from you and Lucas. I thought it would be easy until I met you and got to know you. You are genuinely nice and don't deserve this. I'm so sorry for the way he has treated you and I regret ever making a deal with that hideous monster! I now know the price I must pay to remain a girl is too high. If there is any way I can make things right, I want to help."

"There may be one way to help if you still have my Power Ring," whispered Hailey.

"I have it right here," whispered Tanis as she nodded her head.

"What are you girls talking about?" demanded Rebulus in his gravelly voice.

"We were just talking about school and some of the girls in class," assured Tanis.

"Get your water bottle and move away from that girl," sneered Rebulus.

Hailey screwed the cap back on the bottle and handed it to Tanis.

"Thank you," said Hailey. "You are a good friend."

Hailey's words truly surprised Tanis, but they were the best words she had ever heard. She gripped the bottle and put her hand firmly over Hailey's for a few seconds, but a few seconds was all she needed. Tanis took the bottle and walked back to her seat on the rock. Tanis looked over at Rebulus and saw his sly grin as he looked at her and then to Hailey. Tanis knew at that moment she had made the right decision.

Moments later, Hailey saw flashes of light from the tunnel and heard footsteps she hoped were from Lucas and Damian. Lucas finally came into view with Damian right behind him. Lucas was wearing his green shoulder pack and Hailey wondered if Prescott was inside. Damian walked over to Rebulus and handed him the Power Ring with the storm crystal.

"Lucas, my lad, will you be so kind as to take a seat next to Hailey," said Alastair.

Even in this terrible situation, Alastair still appeared to be pleasant. He sounded like a cultured

English gentleman, but Lucas knew his only desire was for power. He wanted the power of the Sun Stone.

"Damian were you followed?" asked Alastair.

Damian quickly looked around to make sure he gave the right answer.

"No sir, Mr. Janus. I followed your instructions and made sure we were alone."

"That's very good. Will you please bring me the Sun Stone?" said Alastair.

"Um, I don't have it," admitted Damian sheepishly.

"What do you mean you don't have it?" bellowed Rebulus. "Where is it?"

"Lucas has it in his shoulder pack," said Damian meekly.

"*You* were supposed to bring me the Sun Stone. Why does Lucas have it?" demanded Rebulus.

"I tried to pick it up, but it shocked me," replied Damian.

Alastair held up his hand and turned to Rebulus and whispered something then returned his gaze to Lucas.

"Lucas? Whatever game you have planned, is it worth hurting your friend Hailey?"

Rebulus looked at Damian and nodded. Damian grinned and walked over to Hailey. He pulled her up by her arm and spun around behind her and held both of her arms behind her back.

"I'm not planning any game!" yelled Lucas. "I have the Sun Stone right here." as he touched the pack across his chest.

"Then remove it from the pack and bring it here," said Alastair calmly.

Lucas slowly stood up and looked at Hailey. She was held captive by Damian and yet she appeared so calm, without any expression of fear. He was glad for that as it helped to calm his nerves. He unzipped the pocket on the shoulder pack and took out the leather box.

"Please bring it here, lad," urged Alastair.

Lucas took several steps when Alastair yelled, "Stop!" Who did you bring with you?"

"No one!" replied Lucas. "I'm telling the truth. I came alone just like you told me," replied Lucas.

Lucas knew it was true that he had come alone, but he desperately hoped he was followed. Alastair looked around to see if he was telling the truth then he looked up. Lucas remembered that when he used the intelligence power, he would do the same thing. Lucas then saw the little points of light spinning above Alastair's head for a few moments. The tiny lights seem to explode like fireworks above his head and Alastair stared angrily at Lucas.

"I do not like it when people lie to me lad!"

He must have sensed the presence of other Light Bearers. Alastair raised one hand and an unseen power caused Lucas to fly to the top of the cavern. Lucas looked down and wished there was a soft bed below him now. With his other hand, Alastair reached toward the box Lucas was holding. Immediately, an invisible force pulled the box from his hand, and it flew to Alastair.

He handed the box to Rebulus and said, "Now is the victory, Rebulus! Open the box and remove the Sun Stone."

Excitedly, Rebulus opened the box and a brilliant light exploded making the cavern brighter than the noon day sun.

"Eeeoow!" screamed Rebulus as he used his tiny arms to shield his eyes.

Alastair grabbed the Sun Stone and squeezed it until he forced all the light back inside and the cavern was dark again. He opened his hand and instead of the Sun Stone, Alastair was staring at a scallop shell in the palm of his hand.

"You bloody little bugger! Where's the Sun Stone?" demanded Alastair so loudly that his booming voice shook the ground in the cavern. Even Rebulus was startled as he backed a few steps away. The polite and cultured Englishman was replaced by a furious madman.

"It's right here with me where it belongs," shouted Lucas as he put his hand on his pack.

Immediately, Alastair slammed Lucas back down toward the ground.

"Aaaah!" screamed Lucas as he closed his eyes and braced himself for crashing into the stone ground and sudden death. Suddenly, Grandpa Jack appeared near Lucas and stopped him inches from hitting the rocks.

"You're done, you traitorous Brit," yelled Jack as stretched his arm toward Alastair and used his power to bind Alastair with a steel cable. In response, Alastair began spinning rapidly until he burst free from the cable, which somehow dissolved.

"Oh, I'm far from done, old man!" sneered Alistair.

Everyone in the cavern, even Rebulus, backed up and watched, mesmerized, as the two wizards faced each other as warriors in battle.

Jack formed a fireball between his hands and threw it directly at Alastair. The Englishman threw up the palm of his hand and the flaming ball was deflected down a tunnel where it exploded. Alastair returned his own fireball of hot lava toward Jack who caused it to explode into thousands of harmless snowflakes that fell gently onto the cavern floor. Back and forth these two powerful and equally strong Light Bearers attacked one another. The cavern was lit up by exploding fireballs, lightning bolts, and deadly stabbing icicles.

Katrina suddenly appeared and joined Jackson to combine their power. Together, they created an invisible force that shoved Alastair up against a wall in the cavern. He threw his head back and let out an unearthly shriek that seemed to shatter the invisible forcefield. Each time, Alastair found some way to stop or block their power and free himself. And so, the battle went on, but no matter what these pure Light Bearers devised as a weapon, Alistair found a way to stop or block the power and free himself.

Suddenly, Rebulus turned to Lucas, and with a grin, held up the storm crystal. A blast of energy punched Lucas hard in the chest and slammed him against the rock wall. Even though he was dazed, Lucas scrambled quickly to pull the Sun Stone from his shoulder pack. He needed to protect himself!

He created an invisible shield with the Sun Stone that separated them from Rebulus. Each time Rebulus blasted Lucas, the shield from the Sun Stone would light up as it soaked up the energy. As Lucas considered what more he could do with the Sun Stone, he imagined the blasts of energy bouncing off the shield and directing them back to Rebulus. As quickly as he had that thought, the Sun Stone obeyed and Rebulus began jumping from rock to rock to escape the ricocheting energy blasts.

Cunningly, Rebulus saw a way around the shield Lucas had created and aimed above him. The energy from the storm crystal crashed into the rock wall causing an explosion of sharp pieces of rock shards that hit Lucas from behind and knocked him to the ground. As he was getting up, Lucas saw Rebulus draw his finger across his throat signaling Damian to kill Hailey. That's when Lucas realized Damian was still holding Hailey and Damian was protected behind the shield as well.

"NO!" shouted Lucas and he rushed to tackle Damian in a fury that was pure adrenaline power. Damian threw Hailey to the ground just before Lucas attacked and the boys tumbled across the cavern floor. Lucas jumped up ready to fight Damian when he looked over at Hailey to see if she was okay.

A feeling of horror struck Lucas! He was too late! Hailey had hit her head on a sharp rock and lay motionless facing the blue sky through the hole in the top of the cavern. Lucas's heart clenched in pain when he realized he might not be able to help his best friend. Lucas forgot about all the fighting in the cave and rushed over to Hailey. Even the Master Light Bearers stopped their fighting and looked at Hailey and Lucas.

"You lose, Lightfoot," boasted Damian as he looked down at Hailey.

Suddenly, to everyone's surprise, Hailey's appearance began waver and flash in the manner of shape shifting. Surprisingly, she transformed into Tanis.

"Tanis! What's happening?" howled Damian. "It's not possible!

Lucas was confused and moved back from Tanis. Damian dropped to his knees and cradled his sister's limp body in his arms. Her eyes fluttered open, and she looked up at the horror on her brother's face as he came to the realization, he may have killed his sister.

"Why did you do this?" wailed Damian.

With labored breath she whispered, "I'm sorry, brother. But I couldn't do this evil anymore." Her head dropped to the side and Damian knew she was gone.

Lucas looked anxiously around the cave and was relieved to see Hailey and Katrina come out from behind the safety of a rock near the tunnel opening. Damian was sobbing as he hunched over the lifeless body of his sister.

As Rebulus saw Tanis lay motionless and Damian crying like a defeated little boy, he realized his creations had been destroyed. He combined all his anger, hatred and malice toward all Light Bearers and focused on the destruction of Lucas Lightfoot. Rebulus held the Power Ring and combined the dark power from his father and the dark power on the ring and directed them at Lucas, who was still kneeling on the stone floor.

Instantly, Katrina flew to Lucas and wrapped her arms around him and shielded him as she took the full force of the evil power and venom from Rebulus. Lucas looked up into the face of an angel as the shimmering light of her spirit was beginning to leave her body.

"Lucas, I have completed my mission and I must go. You still have much to do to bring the Light Bearers together. You are destined for greatness, and I am honored to have been a part of your life. You now have one more angel to watch over you."

She smiled and softly said, "Goodbye, Lucas, my dear friend."

Lucas felt encircled in the arms of unconditional love for a brief moment, then her shimmering light flew across the cavern and shot straight through Rebulus like a brilliant white arrow. Her light then flew straight up through the skylight and disappeared.

Lucas heard a shriek from Rebulus as he dropped the storm crystal. "No! This can't be happening. This is not the way it was supposed to end." Rebulus coughed as he leaned up against a rock wall moaning in pain with the agonizing thought of defeat.

Rebulus pointed at Lucas and angrily said, "There are others who will finish you. You will lose your light!" Without the strength to stand Rebulus slid down to the ground into an ugly heap of twisted fur.

With Rebulus near death, Alastair realized he was now alone in this fight. He sent one final explosion of energy toward Jackson and Prescott then quickly disappeared down a tunnel causing a rockslide behind him to stop anyone from following.

Grandpa Jack rushed over to Lucas who was still holding Katrina's body. They gently laid her on the ground with her head on a blanket of silver hair.

The Light Bearers looked at Damian who was still sobbing for what he had done to his beloved twin sister. He looked up and saw Lucas and Hailey and wondered why they didn't look angry. All he saw was their sadness.

Lucas knew Damian was being controlled by Rebulus and did not deserve the lies he had been told.

"Damian," said Lucas softly, "I think I can help."

"Damian looked up confused, "What do you mean? She's gone."

"Maybe not," replied Lucas. He pulled the Sun Stone out of his pack and looked over at Grandpa Jack who answered his questioning gaze with a nod. Prescott floated over to Lucas and gently landed on his shoulder.

"Lucas, this is why you have the birthright and the Sun Stone. The greatest source of your power

lies within your heart. I know you will use it wisely," assured Prescott.

Lucas turned to Damian and said, "You might want to close your eyes," as he cupped his hands on the Sun Stone and place it on Tanis's head. The light under Lucas's hands grew brighter and brighter until the entire cavern was blazing white. Within a few moments they all heard Tanis gasp for air.

"You're alive!" exclaimed Damian as he hugged his sister who weakly hugged him back.

Damian looked at Lucas and humbly whispered, "Thank you, Lucas, what happens now?"

Before Lucas could answer, they heard the angry voice of Rebulus.

"What happens now is you die with me." Without another word, Rebulus coughed on his own blood and fell over.

Damian and Tanis were hugging each other when a purple fog came out of the ground and wrapped itself around the twins.

Tanis looked up and quietly pleaded, "Hailey, Remember to thank Miss Harrison and the girls in the class for their kindness and friendship. You are the best friend – besides my brother - I have ever had!"

"Farewell, Hailey and Lucas!" called out the twins in unison before they were completely covered in purple. When the fog disappeared, they had been transformed back into rat snakes. Damian and Tanis raised their heads and looked directly at Lucas then turned and slithered into the darkness.

☼ ☼ ☼

Alastair neared the cave entrance and felt relief as he saw the sun light that would lead the way to his escape. But before he could go further, to his surprise, he was met by an army of angry skunks rushing toward him. Using his power of mental telepathy, he commanded, *"To all of the skunks in this tunnel, I command you to leave now and go back to the forest from which you came."*

One of the skunks stood on his back legs and replied, *"We do not know you. We have received our instruction from our friend Katrina, and we serve HER."*

Immediately, all the skunks turned their backs to Alastair and sprayed their horrible odor at him. Alastair screamed! He could not go back the way he came because he had blocked the tunnel. His only way out was through the toxic stench. He ran forward through the pack of attacking skunks, tripping over them, and stumbling out into the daylight. He was gasping for fresh air and rubbing his burning eyes. When he finally opened his eyes, he was staring at two mountain lions. They hesitated only a few seconds before they attacked Alastair Janus with full force and bringing him to the ground.

Back in the cavern, Lucas asked Hailey, "How did you convince Tanis into shape shifting to look like you?"

With tears rolling down her cheeks, Hailey replied, "I didn't have to. She volunteered. I think she knew what Rebulus had planned, and she gave her life for me."

Lucas looked at Katrina who still had a smile on her face.

"She also gave her life, that I might live," whispered Lucas.

☼ ☼ ☼

Lucas was happy to see all the Light Bearers he and Hailey had visited around the world. They all came to the cemetery for the memorial service for Katrina Wakanda. There was a sadness she was gone, but it also felt like a happy family reunion. Even the weather was perfect. Lucas sat in the front row with Prescott on his shoulder. Grandpa Jack sat on his right side and Hailey on the other. Lucas and Hailey's parents sat right behind them. Lucas smiled as he thought back to the day he met Katrina and how she seemed to glow. That was the day that started it all. That was the day she had given him Prescott.

"Grandpa, why did she have to die?"

"We may never know all the reasons why things happen the way they do. Rather than ask why, it's better to ask, what can we learn and how can we honor her?"

"Well, I learned that Katrina loved me more than her own life, enough to protect me."

"And she still does. She's like your Grandpa Lightfoot and she will be there whenever you need help."

"*Lucas, we have known about you since before you were born,*" added Prescott. "*Because both of your grandfathers, John Lightfoot, and Jackson Rainer, are Master Light Bearers, you were destined for the birthright to keep the Sun Stone and to one day lead all the Light Bearers. Katrina knew that as well and she gave her life to make sure you had every opportunity to fulfill your destiny.*"

Lucas didn't fully understand what that all meant but was confident one day he would. Until then, he would remember Katrina and the feeling of being wrapped in the arms of love.

"*I guess the best way to remember Katrina is to make sure she did not die in vain,*" thought Lucas. In his mind he heard Prescott and Grandpa Jack agree with him.

Hailey then grabbed his hand with a squeeze and said, "Thanks for being such a good friend."

As Lucas was thinking about all the journeys and adventures he had experienced with the Light Bearers, he heard a mournful screech from the sky. He looked up and saw Echo Hawk from South Africa flying above the cemetery. There was another hawk flying with her and he wondered who it might be.

"*Lucas,*" said Prescott, "*If you look up the hill to the edge of the grass, there are many friends who are here for Katrina.*"

Just a hundred feet away, at the edge of the woodland, stood deer, mountain lions, foxes, skunks, and a host of other animals. Perched in the trees were hundreds of Red Crowned parrots and smaller hawks. All were quiet, stilling their cries and screeches to show reverence for Katrina. Lucas smiled and nodded his head, acknowledging their attendance at the service. He was surprised when he heard one of the mountain lions speak to him.

"Master Lucas, we loved and served our friend Katrina. We will now serve you."

With those words, each of the animals bowed their heads. *"Call on us anytime."*

Tears rolled down his cheeks as Lucas thought about the love and support he felt from the animals, from all the Light Bearers and especially his family. The feeling of serenity, peace and gratitude was overwhelming.

Suddenly, those feelings were interrupted by a dark invading impression that caused Lucas to look over his shoulder and down the hill to the cars on the narrow road in the cemetery. There, in the distance, stood a tall man with a bowler hat and dark glasses. He had a white bandage covering part of his face and one arm in a sling. Then, in his mind, Lucas heard a deep voice with a British accent.

"Lucas, even though I was not invited, I am here to pay my respects to a remarkable woman. I hope one day you will understand I am not your enemy, but your teacher."

Lucas suddenly felt cold and shivered. He took his grandpa's arm and wrapped it around his shoulders and leaned next to a true Light Bearer. Lucas then felt the warmth of an unseen arm wrap around him. He knew there was an angel with silver hair and green eyes near him when he heard the soft voice of Katrina in his mind.

"Until all the sinister and dark forces are destroyed, there will be others to take the place of Rebulus. You must continue to stand in the safety of virtue and light."

THE END

About the Authors

Hugo Haselhuhn lives in Prescott, AZ and has a passion to create a positive influence for good in the lives of others. Hugo has incorporated lessons to strengthen human relations shared in these stories and the readers are learning through the eyes and experiences of the characters.

This book series began as a request from his co-author, then eight-year-old grandson, Luke Cowdell, who wanted help in writing a "chapter book". Luke is an avid reader with an active imagination. He is also a deep thinker and asks questions seemingly beyond his years.

Books by Hugo and Luke
Lucas Lightfoot and the Fire Crystal (2013)
Lucas Lightfoot and the Water Tomb (2014)
Lucas Lightfoot and the Sun Stone (2022)
Lucas Lightfoot and the Wind Dancer (20??)

Made in the USA
Middletown, DE
10 April 2023